AFTERMATH

Originally published 2008

This edition © 2015 Dark Star

Text © Brian Giffin 2015

Cover art © Rev. Kriss Hades 2015

ISBN: 978-0-9943206-2-9

Author's Note

I originally wrote this novel in 2008, and since then it has gone through a significant rewrite, mostly concentrating on the first part of the story up until Talon and Tahnee's encounter in Allphones Arena. Most of the rest has been left as it was.

I want to thank Stephen Lord and Karyn Hamilton for reading the original drafts and my wife Courtney for the love and encouragement to release this onto the world. Enjoy.

AFTERMATH

Brian Giffin

Tuesday, September 4

When I finally came to I had ringing in my ears and a searing pain in my temple. I could feel dried blood caked on my face. I sat up quickly--too quickly, and my head screamed at me for being a fool. With a groan I lay back down on the blood splattered, glass covered floor and waited for the pain to ebb away while I got my bearings. My hand went up to touch the bullet graze on my forehead and felt the smooth bump of newly congealed blood. I had been out long enough for the bleeding to stop. There was more than likely little risk of any more danger for the moment, because apart from the noise inside my head it was quiet as a tomb. For some time I lie there pondering what that could mean. Evidently, I'd been left for dead. Whatever had happened to the boys after I'd taken the hit, they hadn't been able to come back for me. At least not yet. Maybe the cops had come in with some more firepower or another mob had come down during the action. It didn't matter for the moment. I was alone, I was still alive and, apart from the graze and the headache, I seemed to still be pretty healthy. After a while lying on the cool floor of the shop, I gradually rose and looked around.

Fuck, the place looked like it was out of a Tarantino film. I've seen some pretty cut up-looking dives, like the Grave Dancers' clubhouse after we pulled the drive-by a couple of years back, but this beat them all. There

7

were bodies strewn right across the street, glass sprayed over the pavement and throughout the store and blood staining the floors and walls like some spastic work of art in brown. Spent casings littered the scene and bullets had taken chunks out of walls and pillars, shattered display cabinets and left large, dark holes in the people scattered in all directions. No wonder the boys hadn't come back to get me. There weren't any left to come back. Cops, wogs, us, anyone else stupid enough to get in the way. By the look of it, everyone still left in town was dead out in the street with a slug in them. It was a fucking *massacre*.

When we heard about the shit going down, we figured that if it was all coming to an end, then we might just as well get in for our chop while we could. Then Pretty-boy hit on the theory that if we got in first, then we could even see it all out. Pretty-boy might have looked like a fag, but he wasn't stupid. We were survivors after all. We played to our own rules, made our own way in this fucked up world. This was our time. A time when only the strong and the loyal and the brave were going to pull through. We didn't have to be outcasts anymore. Now we could be kings.

Ah, but Pretty-boy painted the picture like it was already spread out before us. A whole dead city at our fingertips, with us as its masters. A kingdom, with enough loot and pussy to keep us going for years. He was a poet was Pretty-boy.

It was Gonk's idea to hit the gun store. Sure we already had an arsenal, but if we were going to take over this shitty town, we were going to need firepower. It was just about the first place we'd reach when we hit the city anyway, and if the radio was right it was pretty much a ghost town by now. Even with the world shot to ratshit, some guy was still on air, spinning discs and babbling on, although he sounded like he'd got himself some pretty good trips and had the place to himself. He was putting old Deep Purple records on and singing along on air, coming back now and then to report a car fire or a gunfight before turning the music up again and laughing.

I wonder if he's still on.

The roads were choked with wrecks and pile ups. Botany Road was a fucking mess of twisted metal and broken glass. Dead arms hung from windows and bloodied heads poked through shattered windscreens with glassy eyes. Here and there birds pecked at wasted humanity, and now and then we passed an engine that was still running, bloated bodies of families entombed inside.

Spud and Chook decided to get in some target practice as we picked our way through the eternal gridlock. Heads exploded like vermillion cabbages as they took turns with their shotguns and when we came up against a bus down on Regent Street we popped a couple of grenades in for laughs, and sat back for a minute to watch the carnage. The windows blew out like a big firecracker and rained down a confetti of glass. The whole thing lifted off the road and crashed down again and broke in two.

"Fuck! That was a good one!" Spud roared. Tears were streaming down his face. He reached across and slapped me on the back. "That was fucking awesome!"

I grinned. Spud loved explosions. Once he and I had jumped a guy who'd fucked us over. We carjacked him in his driveway and made him drive out to the back of Luddenham with my .357 at his head. We roughed him up a bit, but Streaky had taken the fall for King once so we'd been told to go easy on him. After about an hour I had the poor bastard grovelling like a worm and decided he'd had enough, so I looked up for Spud and the prick was gone! The next minute there was a dull thud and a flash and Streaky's car went up like a Roman Candle. Spud came out of the trees with tears on his face, laughing so hard he wasn't making a sound anymore, just had this goofy look carved into his face. He said the same thing then too. "Fuck man, that was awesome!"

We watched the bus and the building it had slammed into burn for a couple of minutes, and then King took a big swig from his hip flask. We all knew what that meant.

"Come on you cunts," he said with half a smile. "Are we gonna take this town, or sit around blowing things up all day?"

We swung out around the smoking shell of the bus and managed to weave a bit more freely down the street towards the CBD. The traffic was thinner here. I guess everyone had already split from that part of the world. Or died before they could. There were few signs of any real looting as we came across the intersection with Broadway, but there were bodies everywhere.

Our bikes churned up clouds of birds as we roared across the tarmac. They took off and screamed at us, and Spud shot at a couple of them. As we came down into George Street, there was chaos. There were people around, and they were after the same thing as we were. A big group of about fifteen wogs had smashed a car through the front window of the gun store and were rifling the place. A couple of them on point heard the rumble of our bikes and raised the alarm. Twelve or thirteen black curly-headed heads appeared from inside and a second later some bullets whizzed by. Spud levelled his shottie across the handlebars of his bike and the gun spoke. A kid got the full force of the blast right in the chest and splattered onto the pavement. Pretty-boy opened up with his sub and a spray of bullets danced across the front of the store. Glass exploded with a massive crash and a guy with a red bandana screamed and grabbed at his ear.

"Why don't you go steal some clothes that fit?" Chook cried at them, then lobbed a grenade. It skittered under a black Ford and erupted, taking out another delinquent with a hail of shrapnel. A couple of the bigger wogs taunted us for a second in Arabic, and a little bloke in huge shorts and a singlet took a pot-shot with a peashooter he had. King took half his head off with his .357 and they scattered like dogs. On the other side of the road, some young Asian guys spilled out onto the street from a doorway leading to a flight of stairs. Pretty-boy gave a short burst with his sub and one of them yelled out and clutched at his ankle. The others grabbed him and dragged him back inside.

We left Pretty-boy and Scooter on point out in the street and ransacked the gun store. The wogs had fucked off with a stack of knives and steel and some ammunition and handguns, but it looked like they'd taken mostly useless shit like katanas and peashooters. A few other looters had evidently been here too, but the wogs must've taken them by surprise because there were six or seven bodies slumped inside the store and there was shit strewn everywhere. The place had more guns than the army and more rooms than a block of flats. Chook, Pooch and Chubby went into the next room and for a moment we could hear them smashing things. What sounded like a rack of swords crashed down onto the floor and I heard Chook's Mongoloid laugh as a big set of antlers fell down off the wall and splintered.

"Come on!" King said yelled at them. "We haven't got all fuckin' day. If I know those Arab cunts they'll be back with reinforcements pretty soon. And there's probably still a few cops and shit around trying to be heroes. The heavy artillery'll be out the back. Fuckin' just grab some and get the fuck outta here."

Topper and I went into the back of the section we had first entered and pulled down some Remingtons and a couple of Rugers and Spud led some of the other guys into another room full of old army relics. King and the Doc loaded up with bullets and cartridges and Topper went back into the store and brought out a big case of magazines for the subs.

"Fuck man we should've brought the truck!" I heard Spud say from next door.

"How would we have got it here dickhead?" Toolbox snapped at him and then Grogan laughed and one of them shot something.

"What was that?" King snarled around his cigarette.

"Cunt in here was still alive," said Spud, then obviously to Toolbox: "Well, I guess we just steal one. The streets are full of them. Fuck why don't we take this cannon?"

"Because we haven't got anything to put it in you fuckin' idiot!"

"That's why we need a truck..."

13

"Shut the fuck up Spud! Just shut the fuck up and stop wastin' ammo! Let's just get the guns and get movin'."

Toolbox could fix anything with a motor better than if it was brand new, but his people skills were worse than the guy from *Texas Chainsaw Massacre*. There was some more clattering from the area Chook and the others had raided and a moment later Pooch came back in with a full face medieval helmet on. He flicked the visor up and down a couple of times, then took it off, threw it into the air and shot it.

King had sent Gonk and Eyeball upstairs and we heard them tramping about for a few minutes.

"Not much we need there chief," Eyeball reported as they came back into the main room. King nodded and took a drink from his flask, broke open his big revolver and filled the space in the chamber.

"Load up," he said. "Talon, get back there and find out what's keepin' Topper will ya? I'm starting to get the shits with this place."

I started to head off but just as I turned Topper came up waving a couple of big black automatics. He threw me one and touched his hat.

"Cheers matey," I said and watched him reach up onto a shelf and bring down three more.

Just then we heard Scooter shout and Pretty-boy opened up with his machine gun again.

"They're comin' back King! Fuck there's about fifty of

'em!"

There was a burst of rounds and what was left of the glass in the shopfront blew inwards. A bottle crashed through a pane, hit the big wire meshing and bounced back out onto the street with a loud blast right at Scooter's feet. He howled in surprise and someone took a bead on him and blew him away. From the next room Spud started pumping with his shotgun and I heard Grogan swear. Chook, Chubby and Eyeball fell out into the street, tumbling for cover behind the scattered vehicles. King and the Doc raced to the doorway and crouched there, guns ablaze. The street was swarming with gun toting wogs. The one who'd got Scooter was directly across the road with a shiny automatic that looked like he'd taken it from his mum's handbag. It must have been sheer bad luck he'd taken the Scoot down with that thing. I saw Chubby notice him as he cowered behind an overturned van. He tapped Chook on the shoulder and the big ugly bastard's shotgun splashed the prick's gut all over the rear windscreen. A skinny bloke next to him spun around with a snubnose and started to take aim but Chook was waiting for him too and he joined his mate in the gutter.

Another Molotov came down right outside the shop and a sheet of petrol flame roared up the footpath. There was a crack from Eyeball's Ruger and the big Leb who threw it dropped like a stone, but I saw the Doc fall back from the front of the shop clutching his face and

15

neck. A long jagged shard of glass had torn open his jugular and blood was spurting out like a fountain. Topper and I pushed over the sales counter and hit the floor. From this distance I wasn't going to hit squat with my handguns. I snapped a magazine into the Ruger and took a bead on a fat kid in a basketball shirt who was ducking back and forth behind a taxi like he was playing cowboys and Indians. The shot took the top of his head off and he toppled over onto a guy behind him. I shot him too.

Outside, Pretty-boy was making for the shop, swinging the sub from side to side and skipping sideways. A stray bullet had hit him in the thigh. Gonk ran out to help him, keeping low. He managed to reach him and started to pull him to cover but suddenly there were two sharp reports from somewhere further away and both of them hit the pavement. Five cops had come onto the scene from the railway station and had taken position higher up the street behind a bus. It was bad for the wogs, but it was worse for us. The bastards had us pinned, and now the cops had come into it, the situation was dire.

King pulled back from the cover of the doorway and joined us behind the counter.

"Topper! Go back there and see if you can find a grenade launcher or something. Jesus if we can't fight our way out of a gun store then we fuckin' deserve to be massacred."

He called out to Pooch who was still in the room on our right and told him to keep the cops busy while Topper found a bazooka. There was another blast from the street and a couple of cars exploded as one of Spud's grenades found a mark. Suddenly one of the homeboys braved the crossfire and picked up Pretty-boy's gun. He bolted for cover behind a car with all the windows shot out and maybe spent half a minute figuring it out. From my vantage I could see him, but not enough to offer a shot.

Most of the Lebanese bikers and gang members we'd dealt with in the past were pretty handy with automatic weapons, but this kid didn't have a clue. He made every mistake imaginable. He stood up, swung out and opened fire with a short burst designed to rake the front of the store. The kickback almost tore the gun from his hands after the first shot. By the ninth or tenth he was jumping about like he was working a jackhammer. Each discharge made the gun harder and harder to control and he stumbled over a body behind him. Spud laughed like a moron watching a cartoon. We all fired at once and machine gun boy did the hot lead St Vitus dance and fell down like a string-cut puppet.

Chubby, Chook and Eyeball fanned out from their cover and made an advance on the enemy, moving in short crouching runs between cars with Spud and the other boys laying down some cover fire. Pooch called back that the cops looked to be just sitting back for the moment and weighing their options. From where they were holed up they could have taken Eyeball and Chook quite easily and cut Chubby off from us, stranding him on the far side of the street near the doorway where the Asian guys were hiding, probably waiting for the best moment to join the fun. King and I moved across to Pooch's room to get a better view of their position. It sounded like there was a slight lull in the battle. Either the wogs were regrouping or they were thinking about fucking off. Topper came back at last and shrugged.

"Fuck!" King said. "Looks like we do it the hard way."

He pulled a grenade off his belt and looked at me with a grin.

"How good are ya?" he asked.

I smiled back, took the bomb from his hand and flicked the pin out.

"I'm the fucking best," I said.

The three of them stood and blazed away at the bus as I scampered out a couple of metres onto the road. Bullets started tearing up the metal sides of the bus and windows dissolved in the spray. With hardly a second to size it up, I threw the grenade and watched it crash through the glass and into the dead driver's lap. Then it went off and a blast tore through the bus with a flash of flame that leapt out and took hold of a handful of nearby cars.

I wasn't just the best. With a throw like that, I was a god!

Barely stopping to admire the damage, I hit the deck and scrambled back into the shop. Behind us the battle sounded like it was coming to an end. I couldn't see much anymore but pockets of flame and the black smoke of engine oil. There were still a few shots echoing around and one or two screams. A couple of the boys had evidently recovered the machine guns, because there were a few sharp bursts of controlled rapid fire.

"Who's cunt of an idea was this?" King spat, dropping bullets into empty chambers and glaring in the direction of the doorway where Spud suddenly appeared, bloodied and streaked with dirt like the rest of us.

Across the street, Chubby pressed his hands into his back and stretched his ugly bulk. He picked up his rifle and started towards us.

"Well King," he said, "we got 'em on the ru--"

There was suddenly some intense gunfire and old Chubby's guts spilled out like a tin of spaghetti. We had 'em on the run all right. The bastards had run around the block and come up behind us!

"Fuck! How could we be so stupid?" King raved and was answered by cracking gunfire and a hail of ricocheting shells. Any cover we'd had was lost now.

The angle of attack was drastically changed and so was the method. The wogs weren't just firing off lucky shots anymore. A couple of the older and smarter ones must have taken a few quick lessons from us. Now they gave us everything they had, all at once.

I guess I must have been the first one after Chubby to go down, because that's about as much as I saw. A slug came by and burned a chunk out of my temple. My vision went red and then everything went black. What else happened after that, the dead men aren't telling, but there was enough of them lying around after I woke up to hazard a good guess.

They may have taken us by surprise, but we didn't go down easy. We had an entire arsenal all around us and if I was romantic enough to pretend or I was making a movie I'd have King, Topper and maybe Eyeball blasting away in the middle of a crossfire, getting shot to shit, until the last little homeboy fuck dropped dead. Then they'd look around, laugh and King would take a swig before they fell over too.

But it's more likely that Spud got the shits with being shot at and went fucking nuts with some machine guns and grenades and just murdered everything he saw. He was like that.

Well now I guess I'm back where I started.

I found Topper next to me with half his head missing. King was a few feet away, both hands full of .357 and his chest ripped open by heavy slugs. When my sight cleared I could see Chubby dead in the street with his guts hanging out. I stood up on shaky legs and grabbed a gun rack for support. It was useless. My balance was fucked. I took another step, tripped over Pooch and fell again, slipping on gore and guts and fuck knows what. The noise I made sounded so loud I tensed, waiting for someone to come and finish me off like the poor bastard Spud had executed earlier. I held my breath, but no one came.

I knew then that I was alone for certain. I've never really been alone. When I was kicking around from place to place after I left home, I used to listen to this hard-arse punk song called 'Pointman'. About halfway through, the dude shouted "Alone is the only way to be!" I loved that part. I used to yell it all the time, because I figured I didn't need anyone but myself.

I don't know if the guy really thought being alone was awesome or if he was just trying to be a hard case, but it's bullshit. Loneliness feels like shit.

I began to seriously consider blowing my head off. I scrabbled around for something to do the deed and found one of the guns Topper had given me earlier. I put it up to my temple, stuck it in my mouth, jammed it up against my forehead. But I couldn't bring myself to pull the trigger. I kept thinking I'd botch the job, and be lying there with my jaw missing or a big hole in my face, trying to scream. Maybe I should have thought about eating a grenade, but for some reason I didn't.

Then I heard a noise outside and I leapt up and whirled to face it. The glare from the road stung my injured vision like a bastard. Blinking, I pointed the gun in the direction of the sound and shook my head.

It was a dog, standing over Gonk's body, a low growl in its throat. He'd been licking the blood and was probably about to tuck in.

"You fucking leave him alone, mutt!" I yelled.

I didn't want to shoot at it in case someone heard and came snooping about, but he didn't give me a choice. I squeezed off a round and he fled further down the street. There was plenty of meat around there for him to chew on.

I decided that my brothers needed a better send-off than being torn apart by hungry dogs. They'd saved my life more than once, looked after me when I was inside and watched my back when I got out. Now I had to look after them.

Cautiously, I picked my way through the carnage, stepping over Doc's oddly coloured body in the main sales room. I found them all except Spud, cooling and dead. Good blokes all of them. If they had to go out, it had to be like this!

I went back to King's body and took his flask, then sat amongst the glass, blood and the odour of burning oil and flesh and the trace of cordite and drank. I would have sat there for a lot longer but it didn't take me long to realise that, good blokes they had been, they were dead and it wasn't going to do me the slightest good thinking about what I'd lost. I had to look after myself. I went out to my bike which was still out in the street with the others like faithful horses and checked it over. There were a few nicks from bullets but there was no serious damage. Toolbox always had a bag full of tools and shit strapped to his bike. He wasn't going to need it much in Hell so I reached across and took it and went back inside. Pretty soon I was fairly equipped. I found a big army green canvas bag and tossed in cartons of ammunition, then I went through the store and got myself some sturdy hunting knives and some survival gear as well as plenty of gun oil. After that, it was time to look after my brothers.

All of them were shot to shit. Scooter was burnt and Doc still had a long blade of glass hanging out of his throat. I dragged the guys who were outside, Chubby, Chook, Eyeball, Pretty-boy, Scooter and Gonk, back into the place and lay them next to Doc. Then I found Toolbox and Grogan and brought them out too, along with Pooch and Topper, and King last of all. I pried his guns out of his hands and put both of them in my belt. I looked around for Topper's hat and found it close to where his body had been. It was fine. Not even a hole. I put it on and it fit surprisingly well, so I decided I'd keep it. Never said much Topper, but he was okay.

Grogan had a big crucifix he always wore which made him look like one of the guys from Black Sabbath. He sharpened up the end once and used to go around saying he wanted to fuck a vampire bitch with it. Guess he'll find plenty where he's gone. I took that and some other stuff. I took a little something off all the guys. Just some shit that I can look at one day and think about the chaos. When I find some whiskey I'll fill up King's flask and toast them all.

Once that was done I got on my bike and idled it down the street about as far as my range would allow, turned and looked back up at the mess.

Two Asian guys ventured out of a doorway as I passed by. One had a gun but he didn't much look like he was going to use it. I looked at them as if I couldn't give a fuck.

"You guys better fuck off," I said and flicked the pin out of a grenade. They both figured what I was about to do and began shouting in Chinese before running off as fast as they could go.

I weighed the grenade in my hand, took a couple of running steps and threw it as hard and as far as I could. I was aiming for a pillar in the shopfront to get a deflection inside. Instead, I was a bit wide and it went straight into the store instead.

The explosion caused a chain reaction fuelled by ammunition and petrol fumes. A God Almighty blast rocked the street like an earthquake. The gun store erupted into a firestorm and pieces of glass, wood, steel and brick rained down like a lethal hail, hitting with a series of dull thuds. The buildings across the street caught the fury of the blast and doors and windows blew inwards. With no one left to put out the blaze, pretty soon the whole block was going to be an inferno.

I moved off further down the street with explosions ringing in my ears, every moment expecting an ambush from other strays and looters. The thought of a possibly still very psychotic Spud wandering about somewhere was gnawing at my mind too.

I didn't have a clue where I was going to go. In a handful of minutes I'd lost every friend I had, and now I was alone in a city of the dead. I knew I had to get out, but in which direction and where to I had no idea. I toyed with the idea of heading up to Centennial Park and maybe laying low there for a while, but almost at once I realised that I probably wouldn't be the only one to have thought of that so I rejected it.

So I ended up here in Belmore Park instead. As I came down Hay Street toward the railway I looked south and noticed the old gazebo across the park. It seemed like a reasonable prospect, so here I am. I stowed the bike where it was unlikely to be seen from the road, climbed up and lay down. I smoked a little weed to kill the pain in my head and I guess I slept for a while because the next thing I knew it was almost sunset. Once it was fully night I stole across to a nearby convenience store and grabbed enough stuff to fill a large canvas bag, and this book. I've always been a bit of a scribe so I figured writing would be a good way to keep me from completely losing my mind. I hunkered down with a torch under a heavy blanket like a kid with comic books in bed and started scribbling away.

It's close to midnight now and my handiwork with the grenade at the gun store seems to have started a bit more than just a simple chain reaction. West of the buildings lining Pitt Street it looks a bit like dawn as everything goes up in flames and the sky is painted with an orange glow. There's a similar light in the south where an air liner crashed into the oil refinery late yesterday, but that's a long way off. What I'm seeing only a block away is like the gates of hell coming open. I can't stick here too long, and now I think about it I'm not even sure I'll be able to stay here tonight. I better quit with the penwork and keep an eye on developments.

Fuck, I've written a lot. Maybe someday someone will read it all.

Wednesday, September 5

I don't know what to do. Kelly's dead. Everyone's dead. It's horrible. Everywhere there are dead people like someone took all the graveyards and turned them upside down and shook the bodies out. I don't know what to do now. I've been crying and hiding. I found this book and now I've started to write and I feel a bit better. But the animals are all out now. I don't know what to do. I thought me and Kelly had made it. I thought that because we hadn't died when everyone else did that we could maybe go into the mountains and find some more people and we'd be all right.

But now she's dead too.

It's late now. I'm scared but it's quiet and I think I can write a bit. Besides I can't sleep. I tried to for a while but I couldn't. Whenever I try I just see Kelly getting ripped apart. It was so horrible.

I really wish now that we'd just gone to the mountains like Dara said before she died of the plague.

The plague.

I guess I should start by writing about that. One day if the world comes back together they might need to know about the Two Day Plague. So I'll write about that now, but first I'm going to write about who I am so that people will know me if they ever read this. My name is Tahnee Goss and I'm 16. I live, or I did live anyway, with my mum Cindy in Ourimbah Road, Mosman. My dad hasn't lived with us for five years. He works in a hospital in San Francisco now. My mum's been away in Melbourne for a month, so I've been staying at Kelly's. Until last week I was in Year Ten at Mosman High, though I guess I won't be going back there anymore.

The plague is what killed everyone. I don't know why we didn't catch it, or if we did it didn't affect us. It all seemed to start on Monday morning. Me and Kelly were jigging school that day because we both had hangovers. Kel's mum and dad had gone out for dinner the night before so we'd busted into their liquor cabinet and drank her mum's vodka while we watched some DVDs. We got dressed for school and then went to my house to watch TV and smoke and listen to my CDs. That's when we saw all the reports that a whole bunch of people were getting very sick and then dying really quickly, even before they could get to see a doctor. By lunchtime it was happening to so many people that the ones who were left started panicking. There was reports on the TV about whole families dropping dead in their homes and of lots of people trying to get out of Sydney. A few people said that it was some kind of germ warfare and that some terrorists had let off a bomb somewhere, but a scientist on the news said that there was no germ known to man which could kill the way this stuff did. Then someone else said it was some kind of gas like the stuff some cult used in Japan once. It was really bad because the girl reading the news started getting sicker and sicker and then she fainted while we were watching. I guess she died too. That's when we both got really scared. Kelly rang her house, but there was no answer. She rang her neighbour too, but there was no answer there either.

"I'm going home," she said, and her voice was shaky.

I took her hand and told her that I was going with her. I locked up the house and we went back to Kelly's.

The house was all closed up. Her mum should have been home by this time. Kel took her keys and opened up the house and we went in. We were both scared and worried. I think we both thought we would find Kel's mum laying on the floor somewhere dead. But she wasn't there. We'd seen on the TV how the traffic was really bad with everyone trying to get away, so we figured that maybe that's what had happened. She'd got caught up in the traffic. We couldn't do anything except wait. We put the TV on. There was nothing on any of the channels except news reports about all the deaths. No one could explain it and it was just getting worse. It didn't seem to be a virus or a gas at all. People were just suddenly getting sick for no reason and dying. Me and Kelly both started crying and we hugged each other really tightly and cried.

An hour or so later we heard someone banging on the door and shouting. At first we thought it was Kel's mum, but it wasn't. It was Dara. She had run all the way from her house and she was crying too.

When she came in she told us that her mum and dad and her brother were dead. And at school a lot of the kids and teachers had just started dying in class. She had come to us because she didn't know what else to do. We didn't really know either, but that's when Kelly was really good. As soon as we settled Dara down a bit, Kelly went into the kitchen and started cooking and singing loudly and after a little while we all felt better. But I could tell she was worried about her mum and dad. She kept saying "They'll be home soon" to herself and now and then when she thought we weren't looking I saw her sob so we couldn't hear her. I think she knew they were dead by then but she was being so brave.

Once we had some dinner, Dara said that we should go to the mountains. She said that pretty soon if people kept dying that there would be a lot of disease around and so we should get out of the city. The mountains sounded like a good idea. We made plans to pack some stuff and leave for the mountains in the morning.

I wonder why people always think they'll be all right in the morning. I guess we all like to think that no matter what happens to everyone else, we'll always pull through. Like we're the star of a movie or something. The TV was telling us that more than half the population of Sydney had died in the last eighteen hours, but we sat there making plans for the next day like nothing was happening.

We all went to sleep on the sofa. I was the last one

awake. I looked at my friends sleeping. They looked so peaceful. Dara was pressed up against Kelly like a teddy bear. I put my head gently on Kelly's shoulder and cried a little and I felt her put her arm around me. I guess she was still awake after all.

Kelly and I woke up together the next day. The TV was still on, but it looked like whoever was left at the TV station didn't know how to work everything properly. The picture kept going blurry and the guy on camera looked like he'd just woke up and hadn't brushed his hair yet. He was talking to an astronomer guy who was saying something about a comet. The astronomer said that on Sunday Earth had passed into the tail of the comet for several hours, but there was no way that could have caused all the problems we were now having. Well, that guy might be a scientist who knows about stars and things but I reckon he was WRONG. I reckon he was WRONG because it wasn't until then that all this started to happen and if it wasn't that, then what WAS it then? And why were some people still alive and others dead? I reckon this all happened because of the comet. Maybe there was some sort of space disease in the tail of that comet and when we passed through it we all caught it. I saw an old movie once called *The Andromeda Strain* about a meteor that crashed and all the people nearby died from some virus it carried. I think the comet was like that, only it didn't crash.

Well anyway, that's what I think.

When we woke up Dara was gone. We didn't notice straight away because we just watched the TV for a little while but then we got a bit hungry so we got up to make breakfast and Dara wasn't there.

"Maybe she's in the bathroom or something," Kelly said. "You make some toast and I'll go look."

I went out into the kitchen and made some toast. I put the radio on, but there was only some crazy guy on singing along with the music and every now and then going "Shit! Another one!" and laughing. It was kind of scary hearing that so I turned it off. Then Kelly came in. She looked really sad and I knew that Dara was dead.

"She must have felt sick in the night and got up to spew in the loo," Kelly said. She started shaking really bad and I went over to her. "Tahnee, she was all BLUE!"

Then she cried really hard for a long time. Suddenly she stopped sobbing and just stood up. Her eyes were all red, but she wasn't crying anymore. She turned to me and said, "Did mum or dad call?" and I shook my head. I felt so sorry for her and I thought she would cry again but she didn't. Instead she just stood up really straight and tall and said, "Ok Tahnee. It's time we got away from here. Dara said we should go to the mountains, and I think she was right. Let's get some clothes and some food and get going right now."

Kelly was so brave. I don't think I'll ever meet anyone as brave as her. I don't think I'm brave at all. I think it should have been Kelly who's writing all this and not me.

The bear should have killed me and not her.

We got some backpacks and took a whole heap of packets and tins out of the cupboards as well as a big pot and a can opener and some matches. We put some clothes in on top and left the house. I got some jeans and tops and another pair of shoes and my cargo pants from my house and then we went back down to Military Road and that's when we saw the bus. It was blowing a bunch of black smoke and when it got close to us, someone yelled at the driver to stop. It was yellow and had peace signs and a Greenpeace logo painted on the side. I thought that was kind of funny.

I said to Kelly, "Some greenies they are with a bus like that!" and we laughed. Then the door opened and a guy who looked like the bass player from Parkway Drive told us to get on. He said his name was Tom and he gave us a joint and we went down to the zoo.

Tom said that without anyone left to do the job, all the zoo animals were going to starve in their cages or looters would shoot them and eat them. So we said we'd help them let them loose.

The roads were blocked with traffic, mostly car smashes where people had died behind the wheel and driven into poles and other cars. At Spit Junction there was a massive smash with two buses, a truck and about twenty cars. It looked like a weird sculpture of glass and steel. The buses had crashed into each other and made a 't' in the middle of the intersection and the rest of the

33

traffic had driven into them. There was glass all over the road and everything was charred black. Someone had climbed up onto the wreckage and painted a big "666" on the side of the truck. Me and Kelly saw some skeletons inside one of the buses and I felt a bit sick. She squeezed my hand and kissed my cheek and told me not to worry and I felt better. Kelly was always able to make me feel better. I really miss her. I wish she wasn't dead. I wrote in my other diary once that I thought I was a lesbian because I thought I fell in love with Kelly. Well I don't think it was that sort of love anymore, but it was love I know it.

I had better get back to writing about what happened, otherwise I will get depressed again. Writing all this is helping me. I think that maybe when it gets a bit brighter outside I'll go across the bridge to the city. I can't sit here and just think about Kelly anymore. I have to keep going. But for now I'll write about what happened at the zoo.

Even though we only met the guys at the corner of Ourimbah Road it took ages to get to the zoo because of all the wrecked cars. The bus would stop, some of the guys would get out and move some of the cars and then we would go again. It took ages, but me and Kelly weren't too worried because we were starting to get pretty stoned by then. The guy driving the bus, Mick, put on a really old Metallica tape and blasted it out really loud and this older guy called Kyle handed around a bottle of whiskey. Apart from those guys there was also a couple of girls called Jane and Mandy and another guy called Steve. They were all pretty cool and wasted and Steve said that they'd all been out of it since the weekend. We said that we were thinking about going to the mountains and they said that they were going to Byron Bay, and if we wanted to we could go too. Steve and Tom were from there and they knew heaps of people up there so we'd all be right.

"You guys will be able to stay with me at my beach house," Tom said.

Kelly made a 'wanker' sign and we had a bit of a giggle and then Kyle gave us some more booze.

After about two hours we finally got there. There were only a few cars around and not many bodies. I guess everyone had started feeling too sick to go to the zoo on Monday.

Mick parked the bus and we got out. It was a warm day like the kind me and Kelly used to jig school on. Tom and the others came down out of the bus with a whole bunch of tools. They had a couple of big pairs of bolt-cutters and some big wrecking hammers and chisels and screwdrivers. They also had some big tarps and canvas bags. Kelly and me put on our backpacks and followed them as they walked toward the front gate. We didn't go through the proper entrance. Just to the right of there is a big service entry gate which was padlocked. When we reached the gate, Steve, who was pretty built, used the bolt-cutters on the chain and we opened it and went in. It was pretty eerie there, because there was no one around. I've been to the zoo heaps and it's always busy, so it was so weird that it was empty. Even the animals seemed to be quiet. After a couple of minutes we realised that we were all walking very slowly and whispering. Then Tom said, "Come on, let's get started!"

We walked until we were outside the koala house, then we all crouched down while Tom got out a big map. It was a service map of the zoo that showed where all the animals were kept and all the gates and doors that the keepers used to get into the cages. He told us he got it from some crazy old animal liberationist guy he'd met once at a Greenpeace rally. Apparently this guy was going to break in one night and free some of the creatures because he thought their living conditions were bad or something. Tom said he ended up getting arrested busting into a laboratory trying to rescue some monkeys. I think it was pretty cruel to put monkeys through experiments like that. My science teacher said once that if it wasn't for research like that we wouldn't have medicines to cure diseases. That might be so, but it doesn't really matter NOW, does it? They didn't have a cure for the Two Day Plague.

Me and Kelly went with Tom into the reptile house, while the others went in different directions. Mick and Kyle were going off to open up all the bird cages and things and Jane, Mandy and Steve went to free all the seals and take them down to the water somehow. Tom had it planned that we would let out all the smaller animals first like birds and snakes and stuff and then after that we'd free the bigger ones. He said we should leave the leopards and lions and bears until last.

"Won't they be hungry by then?" I asked. "Aren't you worried they might come after us?"

"Well pretty much all we're going to do is open their cages," he said. "Like we won't be going in to them and chasing them out! They'll work out how to escape sooner or later, and by then we'll be outta here!"

"But won't they just hunt the other animals?" I said.

Tom shrugged. "Probably. But at least they'll have a better chance to get away than if they're just shut up in their cages waiting to starve to death. But most of these animals have been hand raised and probably won't do much hunting for a while. They'll probably just find some bodies and eat them."

He seemed to think that was funny, but I didn't. I thought about a lion chewing up a dead baby and I felt awful but I didn't say anything.

When we got to the reptile house we went around smashing open the cages so the snakes could get out. Tom put his hand into a couple and pulled one or two of them out, but I was a bit scared of getting bitten to do that. Once that was done, we went out and opened all the doors to the cages outside where the iguanas and goannas were.

37

Tom used a pair of bolt cutters to cut open the big gate on the giraffe cage. After that we went to the big display windows at the front of the chimpanzees' enclosure. The chimps saw us and came up to the glass, bashing on it with their hands. Tom swung the bolt-cutters at the glass and there was a dull thud against it and it left a big star shape. Then he hit it again and the glass broke and the chimps ran away screeching and clucking like chickens! When they got close again, they stood and started making some loud noises like they were trying to shoo us away. Tom pulled out all the broken pieces of glass with his hand wrapped up in an old shirt, then he laughed at them and did a little dance with his legs bent and his arms over his head and we ran back onto the main path laughing.

Things went pretty smoothly. It was a few hours later by the time we had finished opening all the cages. Some of the animals must have been getting pretty hungry by then because whenever any of them saw us they came over to us and made plenty of noise. That got me a bit worried about what the meat-eating animals would do. I saw on a documentary once that big cats only eat a couple of times a week in the wild and then just laze around, but I reckon the ones in the zoo would get fed everyday.

We met the others near the elephant enclosure about 4 and we pigged out on a stack of munchies that Kyle had in his backpack. Most of the cages had been opened by now, and Mick and Kyle had freed a whole heap of birds and little animals like the meerkats and echidnas. Steve and the other two girls told us how they'd dragged the seals down to the water on the tarps they had. I don't know if they really did or not, because it's a long way from the seal pool to the shore, and seals are pretty heavy, but it made Tom happy.

Now I'm getting to the really bad part. I don't know if I'll be able to write it down. I've written an awful lot when really I was just going to write about this next part but now that I've come to it I don't know if I can. I'm still so scared and alone. I'm writing hiding on the bus but I can still hear animal noises outside and I'm afraid the bear's going to be out there waiting for me.

We were so stupid to go and just sit around with all those animals roaming around free. We should have just come back here! Why didn't we come back here, where it was safe?

Kelly and Tom weren't even doing anything, just walking along, and then suddenly the bear came around the corner in front of us and got up on its back legs and roared. We all stopped in shock and then Kelly screamed. I think the bear got scared or was angry. I don't know. It just roared really loud and swatted at Kelly and hit her. Its claws were really sharp and when I saw all the blood I just knew that Kelly was dead. Then it got Tom too. He didn't even do anything to it. He just wanted to help it so it wouldn't die of starvation in its

39

cage.

So then the bear came at us, snarling. Me and Mandy were crying and everyone was yelling at it to try and scare it away, but it just ran at us, so we ran away. But it was too fast for Mandy and it got her. I heard her scream and then there was this horrible ripping sound and she fell down all covered in blood. I wish I knew what we did to make it attack us. We all panicked and ran, but it was so fast. I didn't know they could run so fast.

I just know that it killed them all. I just know it.

I didn't really see anymore after it got Mandy because I fell down. I think I tripped over a crack or something in the path, but I fell and I was so frightened that I couldn't move. I thought I was going to die, but the bear went straight past! All I heard was its breath and the way its claws scraped on the concrete as it ran by and I didn't dare move. I was so scared I don't think I could have moved.

I stayed there for ages. I heard more screams and roars, and then after what seemed like hours I didn't hear anything else. I started to worry that maybe a lion or something would come, but I still didn't move. It was only when it began to get dark that I felt that I should get away. I got up very slowly and walked back towards the car park. I saw poor Kelly lying on the ground and I went over to her.

I will never see a more terrible thing in my life. The

bear's claws had torn big scratches down her body and face. I could see bones sticking out and white stuff and I was sick. Then I cried. She was such a good friend. I will miss her so much. I'm going to cry again now.

I love you Kelly.

Wednesday night, September 5

I walked most of today, but I didn't get far.

After I wrote about the zoo this morning, I had some of the food in the bus for breakfast and I looked outside. Some goats and sheep had found their way out of the gates and were wondering about, but I could see no signs of anything else. Then I opened up Kelly's backpack and dumped out all the stuff I couldn't use like her jeans and shoes which didn't fit and her bras which I wish did. I filled up the space with the food from the bus which was the one lucky thing out of the whole mess. I had heaps of food now and wouldn't have to share it with anyone. Then I sat down and had a bit of a cry again, but only for a few minutes. I realised that it wasn't going to do any good sitting there blubbing. So I put my pack on my back and slung Kelly's around my front like one of those baby carriers. It was a bit heavy walking like that, especially up all the hills over here. I kept stopping at friends' houses and different places where I thought there might be people left, but there was no one. My idea was to go across to the city first, but I think it's all on fire. I don't know how come but there's a big cloud of smoke coming up from it like it's been bombed or something. I'm not sure where I'll go now. I just have to go.

It was very, very lonely and weird walking through Cremorne Junction and not seeing a living soul, only cars and buses full of dead people with clouds of crows, seagulls and pigeons circling around. They were picking at the corpses, fighting over them. It was horrible and once I was sick when I came across some dogs eating a woman and a little boy. I screamed at them and tried to shoo them but they just growled and I thought about Kelly and Tom and the bear so I left them alone. I didn't feel like eating after that. I just kept walking, but it was so hard with both packs and it was hot. It took me all day just to get to the Falcon Street overpass.

There are heaps of cars around. They're just not going anywhere. There's thousands of them, blocking all the streets around here, all piled up and smashed against each other. Falcon Street and the Warringah Freeway look like two giant rainbow snakes laying in the sun and glittering. But there's no life except all the birds and a few dogs and me and there's smoke and flame shooting out of the buildings across the Harbour Bridge. It looks like the whole city's on fire from here.

I was going to drag a dead body out of one of the cars, but I've found one that's been abandoned. I'm really tired now and a bit hungry and it's getting dark. There's not any safe places to sleep I guess but at least if I crawl into this car maybe anyone who's around will think I'm dead and leave me alone. I'm a bit scared of meeting other people now. Anyway right now I don't care anymore. If I wake up in the morning, I'll go into the city I guess. If I don't, well, I couldn't really care less. I just wish Kelly was here so we could keep each other warm. It's so cold tonight.

Thursday, September 6

Yesterday I woke to a flame orange dawn and the stench of acrid smoke thick in the air. The stink of plastic and rubber was starting to overwhelm the rotting flesh and a gentle rain of black ash was beginning to fall. Maintenance systems were starting to break down and little electrical faults and gas leaks combined with my over-exuberance with the grenades and ammo back at the gun shop were now starting large blazes all over town. The air rang with the wail of fire alarms and now and again there were explosions as locked-up offices overheated and blew their windows and doors out. I looked up to see smoke leaking from several floors of the McKell Building and then with a loud pop a huge pane of glass was thrown clear and dropped ten storeys to the ground where it hit with a sound like an aircraft crashing.

It was time to leave. Actually, leaving was well overdue. The falling glass raised a black cloud of birds that rose up like angry bees, squawking and shrieking, and I was starting to see way too many dogs and rats for my liking.

I scanned the park carefully while I gathered everything together, rearranged the artillery and climbed down from the gazebo. Even with all the alarms and other noise going on, the roar of my Harley was like the loudest thing ever when I kicked her over and I didn't

45

waste too much time letting her idle before I started moving. Scanning the area for movement, I puttered slowly along the Hay Street tramway behind the Capitol Theatre. I had watched fire rip through here the night before, spreading from building to building like an inexorable disease and there were still plenty of hot spots. In hindsight I guess it was pretty dumb for me to stay where I'd been. If the wind had changed to the west during the night I would have become a human flambé in no time.

As I got to the intersection, I looked up George Street towards Broadway and Tuesday's destruction. The block where the gun store had been looked like photos I've seen of London during the Blitz, the blackened ruins of buildings still smouldering, the street clogged with debris. As far as I could see down there in the couple of seconds I looked, there were still buildings and cars on fire. The blaze I'd started with my grenade had spread like a plague, leaping from building to building along George Street and tearing through everything, unassailed by the hands of man. It had swept westwards and down towards Ultimo and Darling Harbour, ripping through the squalor of Haymarket, eating up the dead and exploding car after car with its blast furnace intensity. The Darling Harbour complexes—the museums, aquariums, shopping centres, theatres, amusement parks, ritzy hotels and casinos—all were nothing more now than fuel for a fire that would never be fought.

I waved a final farewell to my brothers, and then I turned the bike downtown.

Downtown was still burning.

It was like riding into the lungs of hell. On one side of the street, blackened shells of shops, offices and churches threatened to topple into the road and on the other huge spouts of flame leapt from doorways and windows and the air was strangled by thick black smoke. The heat forced me to ride as close as I could to the skeletal remains of the buildings on the west side; I felt like I was going to spontaneously combust at any second. The smoke stung my eyes and scoured my throat and the heat was searing. Vehicles littering the streets were nothing more now than blackened husks with blackened skeletons inside. As the heat had slowly encroached along the street, fuel tanks had ruptured causing sheets of fire to rip along the asphalt and send fiery rain into the sewers. Some of the rumblings and muffled explosions I'd been hearing must have been pockets of gas igniting in the drains under the city and no doubt slowly spreading in all directions, maybe shooting blazing arms up s-bends and sinks and sure to start more fires and blasts throughout the suburbs as well.

But I barely saw or thought of any of that at the time. A

47

big pile of rubble had blocked Goulburn Street and I was forced to keep going, running the gauntlet of fire and collapse for another city block at least. Hardly able to see from the glare and the heat, I crawled along the footpath for fear of hitting something at any speed faster than walking pace. Suddenly there was a massive explosion that shook the whole street and sent me sprawling. I lost the bike for a moment and panic gripped me. Squinting so harshly my eyes were almost shut, I saw the Harley barely a metre away, lying on her side. As I reached over to set her right and get the fuck out of there a storm of debris hailed down about me and I was glad I'd swapped Topper's hat for my helmet this morning.

By the look of it the top half of a building had just simply blown apart. A second ago I could still make out its dark shadow looming through the firestorm, but now it was gone. Driven by uncontrollable fear, I knew only to take my bike and run with it. My clothes were red hot against me and my skin was blistering, but all I knew was that I had to get away from here. The explosion had knocked me down less than fifty metres from the corner; that fifty metres felt like a hundred miles. The bike was so hot I could barely touch her but I couldn't let her go either and I could see my leathers starting to smoke.

But I made it. Liverpool Street was still open, although

choked a little with cars, and I threw myself into it and away from the flames as far as I could before I collapsed, throwing my bike to the ground. Another thirty seconds and I would have been a roast chicken. My shirt had already started melting onto my flesh and the heat inside my pants was intolerable. Screaming, I ran down Liverpool Street toward Darling Harbour, looking either for some water or something high to jump off. I can't remember which. My balls felt like they were on fire and all I wanted was to end the pain. I tore across the footbridge and the paving stones, almost leaving scorch marks behind me and lunged for a pond, neither knowing nor caring how deep it was or what sort of shit had been blown or fallen in there in the last few hours. I slid into the water and felt my head indeed hit something, but my helmet was still on and the blow was glancing. There was a shock of relief from the heat followed by the pain of the water soaking my blistered and peeling skin. I came to the surface, stood, took a couple of steps back toward the pavement and passed out.

My right arm and side hurt like fuck but the damage was surprisingly mild compared to what it felt like and what it could have been. Still, I figured it was going to be another day maybe before I would be able to move too far, which isn't good with the whole world crashing down around me.

That's why I'm still here writing instead of getting the fuck away from this hell on earth. I holed up for the night in Tumbalong Park, which was about as safe a place as I could find with so much fire and building collapse going on. I had to drink myself silly and smoke most of the pot to get to sleep; as a result I don't feel like I've slept at all. Well, I guess it's time to move on if I can. From here I can probably get across the bridge without getting too close to the flames. Have to give it a shot.

Later – Looks like I've made a friend. A kid. A girl to be precise. By the look of her she can't be more than 15. She's just gone to sleep next to my bike. I was watching her for a while to make sure she wasn't just playing possum, but she's definitely asleep now. It may just be my suspicious nature, but I can't get away from the thought that she was headed over here because she saw the bike and maybe figured she was either going to steal it or find some other useful shit laying around. Anyway I think I gave her enough of a fright to put any thoughts of pillage out of her head, and if she wakes up after I've gone to sleep and quietly fucks off into the night then I'm not going to complain.

I doubt it very much if she'll get very far, although I have to admit she's pretty well prepared. She's got two backpacks full of food and bottled water and even a couple of maps and from the little she actually told me when I finally got two words out of her she even had half a mind as to where she was going: west, into the mountains. It seems that she and a couple of friends had made plans to get into the highlands, though what they were going to do once they got there is anyone's guess. The way she's going though I don't think she'll even get out of North Sydney, but I'm feeling pretty damn cactus myself right now so I guess I shouldn't talk. At least she's not half burned to death.

Friday, September 7

I read the kid's diary after she went to sleep last night. She's got no idea how brave she is. Lying down in front of that bear, even without all those other animals around, took plenty of guts. And the way she pulled herself together enough to get as far as she has after all that is better than most adults could do. Most people wouldn't have just sat down after that and written about it all. They would have gone insane! I never figured a Mosman kid could be so tough, but this one's got bigger balls than most of the guys I know. She might have thought her friend Kelly was brave, but she's dead and this kid's alive, and through all this shit that takes more than just bravery. It takes grit, endurance and a will to live like a cast iron bridge. If she knew just how gutsy she was getting through all that shit, she'd probably go into shock and shit her pants.

I'll tell you something else too, I think she's right about the comet.

I remember hearing a fair bit about that chunk of ice a while back when they first discovered it. There was a bit of a scare for a few months because it looked like it was dead on to hit the Earth, but eventually some egghead figured it was actually going to miss us by a few thousand kilometres.

It may have missed, but it looks like it got us anyway.

When I was a lot younger, I was pretty interested in

astronomy. My parents even got me a telescope so I could see Halley, which was just as well because you needed eyes like Superman to see it any other way. Back then I had star charts and God knows what else, and a big pile of books about stargazing. I can remember that one particularly good book had something in it about the Kuiper Belt, which is a cluster of rocks and ice that circle the Sun outside the orbit of Neptune, kind of like the Asteroid Belt of the outer Solar System. In those days they didn't know much about it except that some astronomers thought that was where most of the regular comets came from. A little while ago I was at a mate's place and his kid was on the Internet looking up stuff about the Solar System for a school project. He was at this website which had an entire page devoted to the Kuiper Belt so I asked him if I could read it. Smart-arse bastard looked at me as if he was surprised I could read. The little turd probably didn't have a clue that half the stuff in the soft-core mags he had in his drawer was written by me.

I suppose I didn't really take that much interest in it at the time. It was just that the Kuiper Belt reference had stirred up some old memories, kind of like what's happening now. What I do remember about it now is that the Hubble Space Telescope had taken some pictures of some Kuiper objects and they'd shown signs of a red spectrum. In scientific language that usually translates as exhibiting possible signs of life, and I reckon the fact that they'd found these red spectrums occurring on clumps of ice circling around out beyond Neptune probably made for some pretty interesting discussions once all the data got processed. Well, Tahnee here might not think she's got much of an imagination, but she's damn well intuitive. As surely as I'm sitting here writing this, last weekend man came into contact with life from beyond Neptune. And it wasn't very friendly.

I opened one of the tins of food from the kid's pack, shook her awake and made her eat it while I got everything ready. She was pale and shaking as she ate and it looked like she might be coming down with some kind of fever, maybe a touch of summer flu or maybe a second wave of the Two Day Plague, as she'd called it. Epidemics can do that. They'll come through the first time, knock everyone around a bit and take out all the weak ones, like the sick, the old, kids, babies. Then after a short period, before anyone's had a chance to fully recover, it comes back and kills off a few more. Well, if she was coming down with the space bug, at least I wasn't going to have to drag her around with me. I'm kind've hoping I won't have to take her too far as it is.

So while she ate, shivering, hunched in the blanket with her big eyes looking out from black circles of grime like a raccoon's, I went down to the bike and strapped on the bags and weapons. There wasn't going to be much room for her to ride pillion, but she's only a small kid so not much room was all I figured she needed. I had seen a beat up 250 Suzuki back towards Crows Nest. If it was still kicking and she could ride then I figured we'd commandeer it. Judging by the way the guy who'd owned it had both his eyes pecked out and parts of him chewed off by dogs I hardly think he's going to argue.

I don't even really know why I'm letting her tag along. I'll be held up enough until I recover fully and the last thing I really need is a shiralee. Especially a kid, and a girl at that. Still, she's gutsy and a deadset survivor. Ol' Pooch always said there was a reason for certain people coming together, but as the last time he got together with anyone was a few minutes before he got his head blown off, I don't know if that's a good thing or bad.

When I'd finished saddling up I went back to grab a bite and she seemed somewhat better. She smiled weakly and thanked me in a little voice for the food, but I couldn't help noticing the fear in her eyes as she tried to avoid looking at me.

I asked her if she knew how to ride.

"I used to have a trail bike on my dad's property," she said, slowly and nervously. "That was a couple of years ago though."

"That's okay. You won't have forgotten," I told her. "Did you ride much?"

When she nodded I said, "I saw a bike up the road a bit. When we're done here we'll go check it out. If it's not too fucked up you can ride that."

She stayed quiet while I ate some beans and knocked back some bourbon, amusing myself for a few minutes about the possibility of running the Harley on my own farts for a while after breakfast and saving fuel. When I came back to reality I noticed she was sobbing again, gazing off towards the east. I snapped my cigarettes open, lit one and offered it to her. She gave me a doleful glance and then took it with a shaky hand.

"Still thinking about your friend?" I asked.

"Yes," she said. "All of them."

"So am I," I said. "I'll never forget any of them. But it's no good sitting around moping about people we've lost. We've gotta think about ourselves now, and that means getting the fuck away from here. I should have left days ago. Fuck knows what I was thinking waiting around here for Christ knows what. Come on."

She took a huge drag on her smoke that surprised me when she didn't collapse into a coughing fit and lifted herself onto her feet. Then she bent over and reached down for her backpacks. I copped a quick squiz down her shirt as she did and got a glimpse of a couple of nice little puppies tucked away down there. That's

56

when I first thought that it mightn't be so bad having her tag along for a little while at least. Tahnee has blond curly hair which she's cropped short and a delicate face with a small nose and blue eyes. Nice pins too. If she lives, she'll be a bit of a stunner in a few years. I wonder if she's fucked yet.

The Suzuki turned out to be fucked, but a little bit further up the street was a ute with a trail bike on the back. In the cab were a couple of likely looking blokes with no eyes, sockets crawling with maggots. The kid sensibly stood back down out of the way while I lifted the bastard down onto the road and got it going. It started without difficulty and in a couple of minutes she was ready to run. I helped the kid shift her luggage around so she could ride without too much trouble and she took to it almost immediately. There was no room to get much practice in, so it was just as well. I started my machine and let it idle while she got set, and then we were away, weaving gingerly between the stalled traffic in its eternal gridlock.

Until you see them all like this, it's hard to imagine how many cars there were in this city. They're absolutely everywhere, clogging every artery, choking every street, even more so now in death than they did in life. And their owners, running from something they could not escape, trapped with them forever.

We battled our way down River Road and wound slowly through Lane Cove until we reached Burns Bay Road. It was hard going finding a path through the maze of wreckage and bodies. There were wires down across roads where cars had smashed into poles and I couldn't always be sure if they were still live or not. We went around cars that were smashed into buildings, walls, each other, crushed under buses and trucks, burned out shells, overturned or simply abandoned. Corpses were everywhere, either covered in flies or birds and I even had to shoot a couple of dogs that wouldn't get out of the way. All this before we even reached Victoria Road.

After that the going was better, but still slow. I was constantly on the look-out for any signs of ambush and found myself wishing I wasn't riding such a loud machine. We stopped everywhere we thought we might find something useful that we didn't already have or might need more of – batteries, matches, smokes, water, rice, tinned food. I'd send Tahnee in while I kept point outside. Every place had been ransacked, but there was always something we could salvage. We took a break in an empty house just off the main road and Tahnee had a snooze for about an hour, but when she woke up she looked just as weary as before. A few times while we were there I heard bikes go uncomfortably close by and there were other more distant but just as disturbing sounds – explosions, gunfire.

Finally coming up into Ryde we couldn't go any further. What was probably a massive collision involving hundreds of cars was completely blocking the road. A huge column of black smoke from an enormous fire in the shopping complex was holding up the sky.

We made a detour through Putney and came out near the old Ryde Bridge. It was almost dark by now but I wanted to get as close to the M4 as we could before we called it a night.

About halfway across the bridge something happened that I haven't been able to put my finger on. I got a creeping in my spine and a feeling in my gut that wasn't so much a goose walking over my grave but a herd of elephants trampling it into dust and I almost passed out. It only lasted a split second but it was a bad, bad feeling—a stab of abject fear like I've never felt before. If it was a premonition then Christ knows why I didn't get one on Tuesday morning before we all got shot to shit. Whatever the fuck it was, I suddenly didn't want to go much further and as soon as we got off the bridge I took a left up a side street. I heard Tahnee asking me what was wrong, but I ignored her and just rolled down the street until I found a cosy looking place.

That's where we are now, in a leafy side street in Rhodes. We've been on the move all day, and we've only gone about 10 kays. I could have walked this far in less time! I'm beginning to think that we might have to ditch the bikes and hoof it, at least until we're out of Sydney. We could have maybe made it to Parramatta tonight if we'd kept going, but I don't like the idea of travelling much by night and after that black episode on the bridge I'm not in much of a mind to go any further, although I might scout around a bit later. We'll just hole up here for now. It's not as if we're in a big hurry.

Tahnee's rustling some grub together from the tins she's hauling. After that I might go out and see if there's anything we can salvage from some of the houses around here or hit up Westfield down the street. It doesn't look like it's gone up in flames just yet.

I'll keep you informed.

Friday, September 7

We fought our way through all kinds of traffic jams and piles of rubbish and junk for nearly all today. The cars were really bad around the Gladesville Bridge. It looked like a giant baby had been smashing up all his toy cars. Talon got me a trail bike off the back of this ute that was in the street near Crows Nest with two dead guys in it. My dad used to have one on our farm that I used to ride so it wasn't too hard to get used to. Talon kept on saying that we would have to ditch the bikes and walk, but we always managed to find a little gap that we could fit through. The stink was awful and there were heaps of flies. I've never seen so many. They were everywhere, crawling over bodies and landing on us. I think when I finish writing tonight I'll go into the kitchen and grab the fly spray from the cupboard.

We got up to Ryde and it was fully blocked and almost dark so we started looking for a place to hide for the night. We went up a side street and found this house where we are now.

When we got here it was deserted. It's lucky too because it has bottled gas so the stove in the kitchen here still works.

I guess I should tell about Talon. He's this bikie guy I met.

I knew I should have stayed away from that park. I was so tired after walking from the zoo that I slept almost all

61

of Thursday when I should have been continuing. So because it was so late when I woke up I just stayed in the car and ate some food and decided to save up my energy and really think about where I was going to go. It just seems too far to anywhere when you have to walk and I'm carrying so much stuff which isn't helping. So I started thinking that maybe I could just find an empty house away from everything and maybe grow some vegetables and stuff and stay alive that way. I don't know if I really could do that, but I was thinking about a lot of things and that seemed like a good idea when I thought of it.

After a long time of sitting and thinking I got out of the car and looked around. Right near me was St Leonards Park. If you go through there you get to North Sydney Oval where I used to go with Kelly and her dad to see the cricket sometimes. I thought I could see something among the trees and when I took a few steps further along I noticed that it was a big Harley with big luggage bins on it. It was just standing in the middle of the park with no one around it, so I went over towards it to check it out. I didn't think I'd be able to ride it or anything because it was so big but I wanted to check out those luggage bins. Just before it, where I couldn't see from the road, was a little depression. All I was looking at was the bike, so I didn't see it until I stepped down into it. Talon was sleeping in there and I just tripped right over him. I tried to run but he grabbed my ankle real tight and pointed a gun at me. Then he made me sit down across from him and he just sat there for ages looking at me without saying anything. I thought I was gone and I started feeling so afraid that I started shaking and then I think I cried. All of a sudden he just laughed and asked me if I wanted a smoke. Arsehole.

I guess I should tell about him. He's kind of a big guy, not really tall but a bit built and he's got these blue eyes that look like the colour's faded. His hair's long and wild and pretty dirty, but so is mine now I guess. He's got lots of tattoos and he wears this leather vest with no shirt under it and a black top hat and a big crucifix he said he took from his friends who were killed in a shoot out on Tuesday. Well he said pretty much all his friends were killed then, except for one of them called Spud who I think he might bo afraid of. It's sort of funny that he would be afraid of anything. I know that he scares me. The only reason I don't run away now is because it's dark and I don't know which way to go. The streets are all a maze and they're all blocked up with cars anyway. Even if they weren't, I'd never find my way out of here. He's been nice to me so far, but I've seen the way he's looked at me a couple of times so I'm still pretty worried and I can still remember how he made me feel last night when I thought he was going to rape me.

Anyway, he told me to go make some dinner while he checked out the place. Now he's gone out with a big torch and I'm going to write as much as I can before he gets back. I don't know if he's read any of what I've written so far, but I don't want him to see me writing in case he reads it. I know he's keeping a diary too, which I think is kind of a funny thing for a bikie to do. I want to read it but I'm scared he'll find out. He hasn't done anything bad to me yet but I bet he could if he wanted to.

I'm still not used to all the death everywhere. A lot of the bodies are all blown up like balloons and smell awful and some of them have maggots and stuff. I was sick twice and Talon was a bit green too though he probably wouldn't admit it to me. Anyway apart from that, it was so eerie because there was no life around except us. I was worried that bandits or something would hear us and maybe ambush us but no one did. We didn't see anyone alive, only birds and dogs and rats.

Everyone must have died so quick. We went past a school and there was little kids dead everywhere. I felt so sad. I still feel sad. Why am I alive still? Why should I be? All my friends are dead. My mum and dad are probably dead and all my family. Talon has told me that I have to stop thinking about them now and just look after myself, but I don't want to. I don't want to be alive when everyone else is dead, and I'm so afraid of him. He drinks whiskey all the time from a hipflask and I'm scared he's going to get drunk and rape me or something. Tomorrow I'm going to ask him if I can have one of his guns. I used to shoot on the farm too. Dad used to set up tin cans and bottles and stuff and I used to shoot at them with his rifle. I don't know if I could use a pistol though, but at least I'll have something to use if he attacks me. Or maybe I'll just shoot myself. I don't want to live.

I can hear him coming. More later. Maybe.

Saturday, September 8

It's going to be dawn soon, and it'll be a warm one. The sky's starting to fill with smoke. Right now there's patches of really clear night sky, with the stars startling and vivid now there's so few lights down here to drown them out. They look more like billions of windows with lights in them, like looking at a city from directly above. A living city, not a dead one like this.

To the east, the dead city is ablaze. Across the harbour there's an orange glow like a frozen sunrise, slowly spreading its fingers west and north and sending up a solid stack of black smoke like a pillar holding up the sky. If we don't get a healthy dose of rain pretty soon, the entire Sydney basin will be nothing but a scorch mark. Against the dark sky I can see columns of smoke in all directions, and occasional flashes of flame. Everything is gone to shit now. The sky might be clear now, but with all the burning going on it won't be for very long.

After I left Tahnee, I went along the street and through the park at the end. A couple of minutes later I thought I could see some smouldering ruins down that way. I don't think I got more than halfway across that park before I saw what had happened, and I was damn well surprised as hell I hadn't noticed before.

Sometime during all the chaos on Monday morning, an airliner plopped out of the sky right onto the oil refinery at Kurnell. The same thing happened here, only this time the plane landed on a hospital.

I wrote earlier that the top of George Street looked like London during the Blitz. This looked like the World Trade Center. Even in the gloom the picture of utter destruction and death was vivid and stark. The hospital was flattened. What hadn't been taken out in the initial crash and explosion had obviously gone up in resultant chain reactions and fires. Half-blasted walls teetered on the verge of collapse. Splintered window frames stared out like frightened eyes on a scene of abject mayhem. Glass and masonry was strewn far and wide with the blackened and charred remains of human beings still strapped into airline seats, thrown down, crushed and broken like discarded and empty cans. Not much of the plane was left except for the cockpit and part of the forward section that had been sheared off and fallen onto some homes. One of the engines and part of a wing had smashed onto a group of cars. Other than that, I couldn't see much more of it except twisted clumps of black scarred metal. There was an ambulance flipped on its side with both rear doors flung open. I didn't bother going in for a closer look, but I don't know how long I just stood there, staring like a sinner through the gate of hell. I had plans to go scavenging, but all I did was turn around and slowly walk back.

I must have stood there staring for a bloody long time,

because when I got back, Tahnee was asleep and the clock on the wall was reading near midnight. I kicked off my boots and lay down in the bedroom, looking at the girl in the glow of the moonlight. She looked even younger curled up like that. Very young and very troubled, but very innocent. There was a stirring in my pants as I looked at her like that, knowing that she was mine for the taking and there was nothing she could do about it, but I fought it off.

I sat up after a few minutes, went back into the living room and started drinking, and thinking about things again. Trying to think about why. Why was a cunt like me still kicking when so many innocents were out there, empty shells in the playgrounds of schools like those we passed yesterday.

I'm not a religious man. I lost my faith a long time ago. It was stripped and beaten from me by Baptist fundamentalists. My parents to be precise. They gave me so much of their Bible-bashing bullshit that in the end I just went right off the deep end. Eventually even just the very thought of Jesus Christ sickened me to the core, and I did everything I could to piss off my parents and their twisted religion with its love of violence, bloodshed and genocide. I put a lock on my bedroom door so it couldn't be opened from the outside, and then I just used to sit in there listening to loud death metal. Not just any old death metal either. It had to be nasty,

68

blasphemous stuff like Deicide and shit like that. Once I came home with an Impaled Nazarene shirt on and mum just about had a heart attack. They tried to get in and hijack all my stuff when I was out once, so after that I kept the door locked and used to go in and out through the window. Then one day when they went out, me and two mates sealed the door up so no one could get in except through the window. After that I loaded all my shit into my mate's ute, built an altar in the centre of the room, sacrificed mum's cat to Satan and left home. I never went back, not even to get my telescope. Not that I really wanted it, but it was the only cool thing they'd ever got me, and even then it was partly because I told them I wanted to see if I could see God.

My parents waited all their lives for their Rapture. Maybe they finally got it. Perhaps that's why I'm left here on this hell on earth. Maybe all the doomsayers and weirdo cults were right after all and good old Jesus really was hiding away in that comet, floating all their souls up to him in the wilds of space while their mortal bodies dropped dead down here on the earth, leaving only the wicked behind to fend for themselves. That would explain why the dead have such a horrible rictus of incredible PAIN etched on their faces, and little girls like Tahnee were forgotten. Maybe she just wasn't good enough for God, what with her smoking and drinking and cutting school.

Well God, if you do exist, and you're reading this: FUCK YOU. F-U-C-K You! I didn't ask to be brought into this world to "test" my parents, like my idiot simpering God-bothering mother would always say. I didn't ask to be left here in a city full of dead people with a kid who's only just started buying bras. Fuck you, God.

If I get through the rest of this day without being struck down by a bolt of lightning, I'll talk to you again later.

Sunday September 9

Yesterday was fucked. Me and Talon had a screaming fight when he gave me this little pissant gun and he threatened to rape me if I didn't shut up. Then we got stuck in a gridlock and while we were trying to go around it, we ran into some fuckers that threatened to kill us unless I fucked them all, even the chicks. Can you believe that? They thought they were some devil cult and they were living in the arena and as we rode up near there they surrounded us and took us prisoner.

Well, me and Talon might have had a fight earlier, but then he looked after me like my dad would have. I was really scared because I thought he was just going to leave me to be raped by everyone, but he was really just waiting. He waited until they thought they'd won and thon he fucking got them. The ones that got away probably wish they hadn't fucked with us. If they ever cross our paths again, I don't think they'll get away next time.

It was really bad too because everything seemed to start off pretty good. The house we were at had a pool so we used it as a bath. I was a bit scared to go in at first because I thought Talon would look but he said he wouldn't. Maybe he did, I don't know but I really needed a wash and I was glad I had one afterwards. If he did perve I hope he made it a good long one because I won't be letting him do it again in a hurry. Anyway after

71

that he went and had a bath and a shave, which I didn't think he would do, but I'm starting to find out that Talon's not your regular bikie type of guy. At least not the sort of one that they show on TV. I guess I've never really met a real bikie before but he's not what I thought they'd be like. He writes in his diary heaps and he talks about astronomy and stuff. I also found out that he likes death metal, which is pretty cool too. I'm still a bit scared of him though, especially after what happened with the gun yesterday morning. His burns seem to be healing pretty good too. It looked a lot worse than it was. He still scratches them a lot but he's been looking after them and I've been helping.

So anyway after our good start things went bad. I asked him to give me a gun and he gave me this tiny little pistol that wouldn't shoot your finger off. I told him so too and then he got pissed off and slapped me and called me a really disgusting name and told me if I didn't shut up he'd rape me, then he just went back to packing up. That's when I got really mad. I pointed the gun at him and shouted at him, but he just laughed. I know I should have fired to let him know that I was serious but he just got me so upset standing there laughing and smiling that I just threw the gun down and ran away. I ran down to this park and found a bench and sat down and cried. I must have cried for half an hour solid before I stopped. I shut my eyes and I could see Kelly and Dara and mum and dad and everyone, and all the little kids we saw dead on Friday and I cried so hard I was nearly sick. I thought about my dad who I haven't seen for two years and how he only called last week to say that he was coming for a visit soon and my heart broke and I fell on the ground. I'm thinking about it right now again and I feel like there's a big pit opened up in my stomach and I'm going to fall in.

My dad was so great. My mum was great too but not as great as my dad. He just used to sit with me and tell me things and talk for ages. Dad used to tell me about all kinds of things he did when he was a kid and he taught me all about first aid. We used to do so many things together. We went camping and riding and shooting and fishing and trail biking and stuff because he always said he wanted a son, but a daughter was better because I could do all that stuff and more. I used to think that was so cool. Then sometimes he would even come into my room and sit and listen to Slipknot and Marilyn Manson with me and talk about music for ages. Now he's probably dead like Kelly and mum and everyone. I don't think I can write more now.

Sunday, September 9

After my pontificating yesterday morning, I should have known it was going to be a bad day. God hates me. And that's just fine because I hate him right back. This next bit's going to take a while to tell, so I hope I got enough left in me to put it all down before I pass out.

Naturally, everything started off all right. We grabbed some soap out of the bathroom and used the pool to wash ourselves. I let Tahnee go first and I resisted the temptation to spy on her through the window by using a razor I found in the bathroom to shave. I'm not much for full beards myself, and it felt better to be rid of some of the grime from the past few days.

Tahnee came back in after about twenty minutes wearing some fresh clothes, a pair of khaki cargo pants cut off a few centimetres above the ankle and an Avenged Sevenfold t-shirt. She was towelling her hair off absently as she came in and sat down on the sofa, pretending to ignore me. I cast my eyes over her again and realised that the tussled hair and dirt-streaked face that I'd thought was cute was nothing compared to how she looked all cleaned up. Tahnee is a little stunner, pure and simple. Somehow, I have just got to stop thinking about her too much because she's a really good kid and the images I'm getting in my mind would not be pleasant for her.

I slipped gingerly into the pool and allowed the water to

seep into my wounds as I unwound the bandages. The bite made me wince but after a few seconds it settled down and I was able to relax. As I scrubbed down the parts of me that weren't burnt, I found myself thinking about something other than violating my companion. Instead, I was wishing that it would rain soon, and rain a lot, so that all of the mess out there would be cleaned away; that the slowly spreading fires would scorch and burn all the shit and the rain would flush it all into the sewer, and that maybe those who were left could start all over again, without any gods and governments and corporate whores.

I guess all the peace and solitude of this post-Apocalypse existence is making me soft, turning me into a romantic. Ha. And maybe someone's going to suddenly jump out and yell "April Fool!" too.

Tahnee helped me dress my burns like a champion.

"My dad's a doctor," she said. "He used to teach me little things sometimes like putting bandages on and stuff. You're going to need to keep these on really tight and change them everyday. You're lucky that you didn't burn worse."

Lucky. Yeah, lucky like the guy I saw in a movie once who woke up to find he was the only one in the world who hadn't been turned into a pile of ashes.

We ate out of cans again and just as we were saddling

up to move on she asked me if I had a gun she could use.

"I got plenty of guns," I said, "but I don't know if you can use any."

"Try me," she said. "I can shoot. My dad taught me. He taught me heaps."

I gave that a bit of thought. Her old dad must have been some helluva bloke. Wish my parents had spent one-tenth of the time showing me how to do cool things like ride a motorbike and shoot guns instead of ramming Jesus crap down my throat every second of their sorry existence.

"How do I know I can trust you with it?"

"Because I don't know if I can trust you if I haven't," she replied.

That floored me, although I didn't let her see it. Perceptive little bitch was reading me like a book. Should have known a tough nut like her would be smart as a whip.

"Besides, I need you to get me out of this fuck hole," she added. "I don't know where the fuck I am now."

I took out a small-bore automatic that I'd lifted off one of the hoods on Tuesday and held it out to her. I showed her where the safety was and how to prime it. The rest she'd have to figure out for herself.

"What the fuck am I going to shoot with this?" she said. "Mice?"

I actually quite admire smart-arsery, but for some reason this remark stung like a blow. I guess it was because she just didn't appreciate the trust I was showing by giving her a piece in the first place. She fell down with a yelp as I slapped her face and snapped.

"You wanted a gun, you got a fucking gun! If it makes you feel fucking better, you got a gun. Just let me do the fucking shooting and keep your smart mouth shut or I'll fill it with something you won't be able to spit out in a hurry! You just remember that you might need me, but the only thing I might need you for is something to stick my dick in, so don't start giving me attitude or I'll fuck it right out of you. If you want to get out of this mess without becoming my cum bucket just shut the fuck up!"

I left her sobbing on the ground while I finished getting everything ready to go. As I was packing the cooker into a saddle bag I heard a soft click and, knowing what it was, looked towards where she'd been with a smile on my face. If this had been a movie it wouldn't have been more predictable. Tahnee was pointing the gun at me, trying to aim it through her tears and mussed hair.

"Cunt!" she said. "I fuckin' cook and change your fuckin' bandages and all you can do is fuckin' hit me and call me a... cum bucket!"

The last two words exploded in an anguished shout. If she'd fired, there's no telling what she would have hit, but it wouldn't have been me.

"If you lay a fucking finger on me I'll shoot your fucking balls off!" She shrieked again: "And then I'll make you eat them!"

That was so funny I couldn't help myself and then she was screaming "What are you laughing for?" which made me laugh more. I laughed so hard I couldn't stand anymore. I laughed until I was almost hyper ventilating, and the whole time she was screaming. If anyone else had been around at that moment, we would've been fucked.

Finally she threw the gun down and stormed off. That was funny too, but I was all laughed out by then.

She came back about an hour later, picked up her gun, got on her bike and started it.

"Well? Are we going?"

It was going to be a long day, even then.

Smoke was so thick in the air it was like riding through a fog, except it tasted like ashes. There was barely a breath of wind and the sun was a dull, stupid spot in the sky. The bad feeling I'd had on the bridge began to creep back. Our bikes were so loud and the visibility was so low that there was a good chance we could be ambushed. But there was no question of hanging around waiting for the smog to blow over, and I wasn't about to trying moving on foot just yet either. We had to chance it.

The gloom made it even more difficult to pick our way through the maze of wrecks and death. Tahnee and I kept in close single-file, with myself leading, weaving through the mess, crossing over to what would once have been the wrong side of the road whenever we could to get around some big obstacle like an overturned truck or a multi-car collision.

Then everything fucked up worse than ever, or at least for me since Gonk decided to hit the gun store.

Just before Homebush we hit a wall of traffic that we couldn't get past, like the one the day before at Ryde, and we'd only gone about three or four kays by then. I couldn't believe that after all the mess we'd already seen there would still be so many cars left. It's almost as if all the cars with owners weren't enough and all the others from car lots and garages had just started up by themselves and joined the exodus for the hell of it.

I had seriously wanted to get on the freeway here, but we couldn't even get to it. The smog was so bad I couldn't tell how deep the wreckage was either, but the dead grey shapes faded off into the middle distance at least.

That was when I made a bad call. An outright shithouse call.

I still wanted to get onto the motorway. There were a couple of ways through from where we were.

Parramatta Road was likely to be as badly cluttered as the road we were on, or maybe worse. The other way was through Olympic Park. That might mean we'd have to go right by the jail, and that concerned me a little. Even a small group could turn a place like that into a fortress and hold out for months. But Olympic Park was wide and open and there wasn't much there except for a few stadiums and exhibitions halls that only got used a few times a year so I figured it would be pretty empty and allow us to get further faster.

I've never been a great gambler.

After a few minutes, we were rolling up Australia Avenue toward the place where the Five Ring Circus had once come to town. We should have been able to just follow it right through, but just as we reached the little business district there was another jumble of wrecks strewn all over the road - jam of cars, a couple of burnt-out buses and a truck - and we were forced to swing left down by the railway station. After a few metres I stopped to check the GPS I'd swiped from a car yesterday, and then we rolled forward again, very slowly.

That's when it happened.

I'll say this for the bastard: he was quick. Before I could react, he leapt out from behind a car, grabbed Tahnee's backpack as she puttered by and hauled her right off the bike. The pair of them hit the ground in a tangle of arms and legs; if there was anything lucky about it, it was that she was barely moving or they both would have been hurt pretty badly.

Suddenly kids appeared from everywhere. And I mean kids. Schoolies, still wearing bits and pieces of what appeared to be some kind of private school uniform. There were a couple of girls and twelve or so boys. About four of them had guns. The rest were armed with pieces of wood, iron bars and other junk. They were all about fifteen or sixteen, tops. Evidently they'd managed to dig up a bullhorn from somewhere, because the next thing I heard was a teenage voice telling me to turn off my bike and dismount like some kind of kid cop.

I looked around me and saw through the smoky gloom two figures come out from the gap between two office buildings on my left. One was using the hailer, a shorter kid next to him had what looked like a rifle pointed in my direction. From that distance and with the poor visibility, I was betting that if he did shoot, he was more likely to hit one of his mates if he hit anyone at all. Still, the way things were going, he could very well have pulled a lucky shot, so I handed over the shotgun and both of King's pistols. Then they made me stand there while they went through the saddle bags and unloaded everything into some big Hessian sacks. For a second I thought one of them was going to jump on the bike and try to start it and I got ready to dive as far

81

away as I could, but none of them did and after a few minutes they marched us along the concourse and into Acer Arena, or whatever it's called now - though they doesn't actually matter anymore. Once we got there, a skinny little shit with a machete told us we would have to be blindfolded. Tahnee spun around and looked at me, and I just looked back, shrugged, and laughed. I let her see me point at my boot and while I'm not entirely sure she got my drift she knew I had something up my sleeve and let them bind her eyes. I did the same and we were led into the building. When they finally stopped jostling us up stairs and along passageways, I was shoved into a room and my blindfold was taken off. I was in some kind of booth high above the arena. Tahnee had evidently been taken to another room, and it didn't take too much imagination to picture what some of these losers may have had in mind.

After what seemed like several hours, during which time I could hear Tahnee crying in the next room, the door opened. I noticed a kid with a rifle step back as three others filled the doorway. A dumpy chick with big tits and a face like a snow plough, a scared-looking Asian kid with glasses and a tall skinny guy about seventeen came in. The first two were carrying guns and the skinny guy had a beer. He offered it to me. I was surprised to find that it was reasonably cold. As I cracked the top and took a swig, he pulled up a chair, swung it around and then sat down on it back-to-front like a high school tough guy.

He told me what his name was, but I didn't take any notice because I'd already decided I was going to call him Snowy. He'd probably been called that a lot at school and hated it, so it was a good name to use if I needed to use one.

He was a weedy little punk with dead white hair that he'd cut into the parody of an old-style crew cut sometime in the past couple of days, probably without the aid of a mirror or, by the look of it, a decent pair of scissors. Or maybe the stupid-looking bitch with big tits had done it by sticking his head up her snatch and flexing.

"Glad you could both drop by," Snowy said. "I wondered how long it would be before we had visitors to our little shrine here. We've been quite busy getting it all ready, you know. There's a huge amount of room here for our little community, plenty of area for expansion. What do you think of the place?"

He went on like this for a while, as if he was some kind of upper class criminal mastermind from a James Bond film. The big-titted bitch kept giggling every now and then and he'd smile as he went on with his self-indulgent prattle. I was beginning to wonder how much longer I was going to be able to restrain myself from cracking his skull open with the empty beer can I had when he finally finished, waiting for some kind of response.

"Got any more beer?" I asked, as if I hadn't been listening. Which was true.

He looked at me for a long moment and then laughed, stood up and started poncing about the room. I thought he was going to start carrying on like Blofeld again, but instead he sat back down and looked at me sternly.

"You haven't heard a word I've been saying have you?" he said. "You know, I thought you'd be the type of man who'd jump at the chance to be a part of our little society. Maybe even help me lead them. We've got beer, women. You would be a king among men."

"Not interested," I told him flatly.

"I see." There was a hint of anger in his voice now. "Well, perhaps after we've finished with your girlfriend, you might decide to change your mind."

I grunted.

"Be my guest. I'm just about through with dragging her around with me anyway. You could pass her around like a bong at a hippie fest for all I could give a fuck."

"You know, I don't buy that," Snowy said. "You bikies don't like to share your women, especially a babe like her. Why should you want to give up this little honey? I wouldn't."

"Well you ain't me," I growled, though inwardly amused that he knew so much about 'bikies'. I guess

84

he'd spent an afternoon once watching Stone while he hid at home from the schoolyard bully. "And she ain't my woman. Just some dumb kid I found. I don't give a fuck what you do. I just wanna get out of this hellhole so I can breathe the air without choking on ashes."

"If you insist," the prick said in his infuriatingly frustrating way. "If you're good we might give her back when we've finished. That is if she behaves herself so we don't have to kill her."

"Like I give a shit," I told him.

He just smiled like an arrogant prick and nodded to the kid by the door. The kid nodded back and came inside. Snowy told him to stand guard and then he and the others left. The new kid did some stupid salute and took up a position like some incidental prison guard character in a bad movie. He looked at me with a glare that was trying to be steely, but I just looked back and he turned away towards the window.

A minute or so later I saw four of them drag Tahnee past the doorway. I caught a glimpse of her terrified face as she was hauled by. Her eyes bore straight into my soul.

I sat quietly for about five minutes and then I spoke.

"Hey kid," I said to the guard.

He looked over but was smart enough not to actually come closer.

"What are they gonna do to her?"

I already had a pretty good idea, but I had to distract him somehow.

"Initiation," he said, as if that was an answer.

"Initiation into what? What do they do?"

The kid relaxed a little. He must have felt some kind of importance to have been assigned to look after me. I dare say I was the biggest (and probably the only) threat they'd ever faced since they'd set up their little enclave here a few days ago and he was probably feeling pretty cocky that he'd been chosen as my guard.

"Into the brotherhood. She'll only be the second one we've done this new way. We had to do it differently before because of the cops and shit, but now we can just do it the way it was supposed to be done."

"So what happens?"

"She gets tied up and we all take turns, then we brand her arse with the Clan Mark."

Well surprise, surprise. What an original idea. I wonder where Snowy came up with that one. Sounded like a story I'd written for *People* once about some dumb 'Satanic sex cult'. We hadn't had a lot of details about it, just some blurry pictures of some fat-arsed naked sluts and a photo of a dude who looked like an anaemic Aleister Crowley, so I'd just made most of it up.

I laughed. So did the kid.

Then he looked at me with an earnest look on his face, as if he was about to apologise for being a dumb fuck with less than a minute to live.

"Course we only do the chicks that way," he said. "The guys have to do other shit like walking on hot coals and shit."

I nodded. At least they weren't a bunch of homos. Not that it would matter if they were or not.

"Don't you get a go?" I asked.

"Yeah," he said noncommittally. "I went first last time, so I go last this time."

"That's some bad slops!" I said with a grin.

"Ha! Yeah it is hey!" the kid agreed with a laugh, and then I shot him.

The small bore I had in my boot didn't make a lot of noise and didn't have much guts but I'd modified the ammunition a little. The entry wound was small but once it hit the shell exploded and the wall behind the kid suddenly got a vermillion paint job. He just had time to register the shock on his face before he fell into a heap. I leapt forward and snatched up the rifle. It was a semi-automatic hunting piece. In the gloom I checked the magazine. It was full. As an after thought I also checked the safety. It was on. I punched myself in the head at the knowledge that I could have done the cunts over in the first place, then I moved on toward the arena.

Inside the vast main room it was dark as a cave except for the area in the very centre of the floor which had been cleared of all the concert seating, leaving only the bare concrete. The kids had built a fire at one end and were standing in two rows down the middle, each one holding a candle. There was an altar made out of old furniture at the opposite end and Tahnee was spread over it with some kind of sheet or tablecloth over her. They'd gagged her securely but she was flailing about in whatever restraints she'd been put in. Snowy was standing behind the altar next to a barbecue with a long iron rod resting in it. Except for him, all the kids were naked and facing away from me. I noticed a tall, willowy chick with some kind of round purple mark on her arse and figured she must have been the other recent 'recruit'. They were all chanting something stupid that sounded like it had been made up while watching the original version of *The Wicker Man* at a drug party. Still, it was pretty well organised so I'm guessing some of them at least had been running this little cult for some time. Who knows what sorts of shenanigans take place in exclusive private schools?

While it was only small, the fire was the only light in the whole room so it brightened the floor area quite satisfactorily. I crept down between the silent rows of seats until I was just outside its orange glow. I levelled the rifle across the back of the chair in front and lined up the last kid in the right hand row. Then I flicked off the safety and fired.

There was chaos after that.

The bullet went straight through the first kid and into the second. They collapsed forward onto the third in line, who screamed like he was being anally raped. Of the rest, some started to scatter into the darkness. Others just stood rooted and terrified to the spot, looking around like startled rabbits. I picked off three more of them before they got the message and bolted. I was somewhat amused to see that one of those I'd nailed was the big-titted bitch with the snow plough face.

Snowy dropped whatever it was he was reading from, which was probably a collection of Lovecraft stories judging by the bullshit he'd been saying, and hunkered down behind the altar.

"Stand up you spineless little cunt!" I shouted at him. "Don't try to get away from me! If you try to run anywhere I'll see you, and if I see you I'll blow your fucking head off, so you better stand up right now!"

I moved along the seating rows so that I came around towards the altar at a high angle and hidden in the darkness. I wasn't sure if any of the dipshits I'd shot at had thoughts of coming back with weapons to the defence of their glorious leader or if they'd just fucked off for good, so I wasn't about to go down to where I could be seen easily. I was pretty sure it was the latter, but there's always a chance someone will try to be a hero.

Terrified voices and crying echoed through the complex. The kid who'd fallen under the first two I'd killed was still lying on the floor, sobbing loudly. I told him to shut up and I watched, barely able to stop myself from laughing, as he twisted his face up and bit his lip. Now he looked like he was being anally raped as well.

I shouted for Snowy to stand up again, and this time he did. With a machine gun. Where it had come from I couldn't say, but just like my mate from a few days ago, he'd never fired one before in his life either.

"I'll kill her!" he screamed, pointing the weapon at Tahnee. I heard her wail through the gag as the muzzle waved at her face.

"I told you I don't care!" I shouted back.

I knew what he was going to do then, and I merely waited. He whirled toward the sound of my voice, but in a huge room that was practically empty like this, my shouts were bouncing all over the place. Still, he was surprisingly accurate about my location. I watched him pause for a second, aiming for a spot only six seats away from where I was hiding. Like the movie star he so desperately thought he was though, he fired one-handed. The gun leapt about in his half-arsed grasp like he'd just touched a million-volt cable and he dropped it, but not before the kickback from twenty or so rounds had sent him reeling backwards. He toppled against the barbecue and knocked it over, sending a shower of red hot embers over the floor, which he consequently then slipped on and fell into. Had he been able to, he would have screamed, except he'd smashed his head open on the playing surface and knocked himself out.

Two seconds later the robe he was wearing erupted like a Roman Candle. I waited briefly to see whether His Holiness would suddenly leap to his feet and start flapping about like a bit actor from a disaster film, but he didn't. As it turned out, Snowy-boy had actually cracked his scone pretty hard when he'd fallen and even if he hadn't caught fire he would have died very quickly anyway.

It was quiet in the arena now except for Tahnee's muffled cries and the whimpering naked cult member. I shouted at him to get up, and he did, nervously excavating himself from the tangle of bodies he'd fallen under. Covered in blood and sheet white from fear, he stood on the court with his knees together and tears rolling down his face. He looked around for a moment for something to put on.

"Untie her!" I yelled.

He nodded and stumbled toward the altar, tripping over the plough-faced slut. He fell, screamed and scrambled back to his feet, then ran the last few feet with his eyes screwed shut. After a few minutes fucking around, he finally got Tahnee untied, and she sat up with a flurry

91

and punched him hard right in the stomach. Before I could stop her she was screaming at him and kicking the shit out of him. I had to go down there and drag her away, but she actually broke free and starting attacking him again.

Tahnee had finally snapped, had finally been pushed over the edge. What she had been only minutes away from enduring was not lost on her and her fear and rage had found a vent. She kicked the naked boy viciously in the face, neck, chest and balls, spat on him and screamed, laughing and crying at the same time. I was almost expecting her to shit and piss on him as well when she just as suddenly stopped, stood stock still and then collapsed.

I caught her just in time.

The small fire that had been Snowy flared briefly and then went out. The stink of his flesh and hair was vile. I threw Tahnee across my shoulder and carried her away from the arena toward the room I'd been held in. The naked kid I just left on the floor, bleeding and moaning like a run-down dog. He probably didn't really deserve it, but I didn't care, and I still don't.

I laid Tahnee down on the floor away from the door, then closed it as I went back into the hall. I didn't have to search long for our gear. The kids had stowed it in another room a little further down the corridor. They hadn't even gone through it. We had canvas bags and backpacks full of hardware, ammunition and supplies, and they didn't even look inside. All they'd been able to think about was how much fun they were going to have "initiating" Tahnee into their "cult".

A few weeks ago, I probably was the same way. But back then I didn't have to worry that much about how I was going to make it through until tomorrow without the luxuries of 21st Century living. If I'd known this shit was going to come down, I would have started hoarding tins of beans and boxes of shells years ago and gone to live in a concrete bunker somewhere with a sly grog still and a few hundred gallons of metho and some porn.

When I got back to our room I barricaded the door closed and lit some of the candles that I had found laying around the place. The kids seemed to have had a pretty good supply of them. I set a few up around the place, standing them in their own wax away from anything they could burn and in a few minutes there was a nice glow in the place. Then I rolled out a blanket for Tahnee. I'd found her clothes in the room next door where they'd kept her after we'd been brought here, so I dropped them down beside her so she could find them when she woke up. Her faint had passed and she was now completely asleep, deeply and comfortably. The furrow was gone from her brow and the raspiness that she'd picked up in her breathing seemed to have passed too. I sat down where I could watch both her and the door and started drinking.

Well, I didn't touch her, but after a while I got down next to her on the floor and whacked off, and for some reason my mind conjured a nasty image of the plough-faced slut taking my load in the face while she tried to struggle out of a pair of really decent handcuffs.

I actually felt better for having a wank and I drifted off to sleep pretty good after that. It was the best night's sleep I've had in a while too.

I've written a fucking lot here. It's early afternoon and Tahnee's been slipping in and out of sleep like she's in some kind of fever. I checked her out, but her temperature's normal, so I'm guessing it's just a case of severe exhaustion brought on by terminal stress. She is just a kid after all. And we're going to have to hoof it from here. The kids have fucked off but a couple of them tried to mess with the bikes when they left. I scouted around a little earlier and the bikes were blown to shit. The booby trap I set must have been triggered by some of them after I went to sleep last night. Took a couple of them out too, and I guess it must have finally scared them off for good. The kid Tahnee beat up wasn't around when I looked for him either, and I didn't find him holed up anywhere, so I think that for the moment we're alone here. When Snowy was giving me his welcoming speech I found myself wondering why they

they'd set up their little enclave here and not at the Novotel down the road, but I've since learned that's because the place is nothing but a smoking ruin.

Once it hits dark we'll make a move. Now that we're on foot darkness will be the time to travel. At least I won't have to worry about the noise of our bikes alerting someone to our presence anymore.

Tuesday, September 11

I'm not going to write much today. I'm still tired and I feel sick. All the smoke in the air is giving me bad asthma and I coughed up green stuff before. It's cool staying here where we are at the moment but I don't think Talon will stay much longer and I want to go soon. If I stay under this smoke for much longer I'm going to choke. It's still daylight now but you can't tell because of the smog.

For the last two nights we've been walking. Our bikes got fucked up by the dickheads at Acer so we've had to walk ever since. I never knew Sydney was so big.

Just a few minutes ago I read back the first part of the diary when me and Kel and Dara were going to try and reach the mountains by ourselves. Well we wouldn't have made it even half as far as me and Talon have come. We probably would have ended up doing what the guys who let us stay with them here did and just found a place that was half-decent and tried to live there.

They're pretty cool. There's four guys and three girls all living in this big double-storey house that they've made up like a castle with barricades and stuff everywhere. Talon said that they are mostly pretty smart. They have made a vegetable garden and a generator for power and a couple of big radios that they listen to and two big dogs.

96

We met them just after we went into a supermarket to get some more supplies. There was a guy sitting out of the front of it when we got there, but he killed himself just after we went inside. Talon said that he was sick and would have died soon anyway, but I wish he would have waited until after we left because he shot himself in the head and it made me throw up.

Well after that we walked about two streets away and met these two guys. It was still pretty early in the morning and we were looking for somewhere to sleep. We sort of surprised each other. They were walking down one street with one of the dogs and we were going down the other and we both came around the corner at the same time. At first they were pretty scared and we all just stood there for ages looking at each other. I kept looking at Talon to see what he was going to do, then one of the guys called Pete just said really nervously, "Have you got any smokes?" and Talon gave him one of the packets he had and everything was cool after that.

They were cool and they've let us stay overnight and fed us and right now he's out with one of them looking for stuff to help them strengthen the defences around their house a bit because he thinks that they might need it if someone did attack them. I'm just sitting up here inside their messy living room for the moment heaving. One of the girls, Michelle, gave me a Coke which is cold. I never thought I would want a Coke so bad. She gave me an asthma puffer too but it's not doing very much.

I hope it rains soon. When it does I think I'm going to go stand out in it and get soaked. While we were walking last night, Talon said something about dew. We were cutting through this park and I guess it was about 4 or 5 in the morning. Talon was looking at the trees and then he looked over at this car parked nearby and said "Don't you think that's weird?"

"What's weird?" I said, and he pointed at the windows of the car.

You know how early in the morning, car windows get foggy from dew? Well there wasn't any. I think it's because the smoke is so thick. It's sure been pretty warm for the past couple of nights, almost like during the day. I mentioned that to Talon and he said it's like the greenhouse effect. He explained that Sydney is in a big river basin and all the smoke is collecting there and just hanging around, and because its so low and thick the warmth can't get out. When it finally does rain, I hope it rains and rains and rains for days.

Well that's enough writing. I just coughed my lungs up again so I'm going to try and sleep for a while. I hope I don't have nightmares again.

Wednesday, September 12

For the last couple of days we've been holing up in a house with a group of young guys and girls. They're set up pretty well, but as soon as it's dark tonight I'll be moving on. Things might begin to get a little complicated if I stick around much longer. I don't know if Tahnee wants to come with me, but the way the smoke and crap in the air is making her cough I reckon she'd be a fool to stay here.

There's a thick grey haze in the sky now, spreading in all directions. Looking out from the front balcony of the house, it looks like there might be a blanket of thunderheads coming in from the southwest, but the smog is too thick for me to be able to tell for sure. We could do with some rain. It's bizarre that we haven't had any since the plague.

We met the first two of the guys quite suddenly and there were a few long, tense seconds before the shorter one just flicked his hair out of his eyes and said, "Have you got any smokes?"

I almost burst out laughing. We'd been standing there facing off for a minute or so and then he says that! It was the second time in less than an hour that someone had asked us the same thing.

I have to say that I was actually pretty relieved. Tahnee and I had been walking most of the night and were looking for a place to rest up for the day when we bumped into this pair of jokers with a big black Shepherd on a chain, just walking down the street like they owned it. Although I guess given the current circumstances, they pretty much did.

We probably wouldn't have been there at all except that Tahnee wanted to get tampons. I reckon I should have known that would come up sooner or later. The good thing about it though was that it made me think about doing some serious requisitioning for the rest of the trip. I thought briefly about ransacking a few houses, but I figured that would be pretty much a hit and miss type effort and would most likely take a bit too long. We hadn't exactly been dragging the chain since we left Homebush, but I wasn't about to waste a couple of hours ratting through a whole street's worth of houses for a few tins of baked beans and some Tampax.

Luckily by this stage I had a vague idea of where we were in relation to the nearest supermarket, and we got there just as the sun was rising, although with the smog from all the fires so thick in the air we only knew it was sun up because the sky went from dark grey to a not-so-dark grey.

The place stunk to high heaven of course. It was a sour, rubbish tip smell that was mostly rotten meat and fish as if some disgruntled garbage truck drivers had dumped their loads in the street. Almost as bad was the stink of the old guy sitting on a milk crate near the door, surrounded by empty tins and bottles. He must have been living on nothing but baked beans and whiskey for the past ten days and he obviously didn't care too much about where he took a shit. There were little piles of it all over the place like a minefield. Tahnee wrinkled her nose and looked like she was going to pass out.

"Do we have to go in there?" she asked, and I was half-wishing we didn't.

"We could find another one, but it won't be much different. They're all gonna stink like hell."

"What about that guy?"

"What about him? Doesn't look like he could give a shit and if he does… Well…" I shrugged.

Tahnee nodded and followed me gingerly.

About twenty metres from the doors the old guy looked up with a jerk, squinted out of one eye and cracked a smile that showed about three teeth clinging desperately to some badly swollen gums. He was a long-time derro. He wasn't old at all, and wasn't ever going to be. If he didn't get something other than tinned beans in him soon, he was finished.

"Well hello there!" he shouted, waving his arms around like a marionette. "Got some pretty good specials inside! Got all sorts of good bargains! Got some pretty cheap meat goin'!"

He exploded into an insane cackle that nearly shook the

last of his teeth out, then stopped and coughed up some black shit that looked like road tar. Tahnee went to scoot past him but even before he'd recovered from his fit his hand shot out and grabbed her pants leg.

"Gotta pay the toll girly!" he slurred. "Gotta gimme a kiss first!"

She broke from his grip with barely an effort and took a half step backward toward me. To my sheer surprise she pulled the gun out of her pants and pointed it straight at him.

"How about I just blow your fucking head off?" she said. I would have burst out laughing except that her tone was so earnest I thought for a second she'd snapped again. I remembered that she was probably pre-menstrual and knew that could totally fuck with some women; for a moment I figured that letting her have a gun at this time of the month was not a good idea, and took a mental note of what the date was.

The guy sobered up instantly and stared at the gun barrel as if it were salvation. I don't know if he knew he probably had scurvy or not, but he knew he was going to be dead pretty soon.

"Why don't you?" he said. "Do me a favour. Ain't nothin' to do but sit aroun' an' wait anyway."

I reached over and moved the gun away. We had far more use for bullets than to waste them on this sack of shit.

"Least tell me y' names," he protested. "Got any smokes?"

"Talon," I said, ignoring his question. "This is Tahnee. Now if you've got no objections, we'll just do our shopping."

"Tahnee and Talon!" the old young drunk shrieked, laughing again suddenly. He spat into his palms and rubbed his hands together. "Sounds like a poem to me!"

"It's more like a fucking nightmare," Tahnee said bitterly, and I had to smile in spite of myself. The drunk laughed so hard he couldn't make a noise anymore and promptly fell off his milk crate and onto the pavement into a pile of his own shit.

We walked past him and through the doors and both of us almost passed out. The reek was intolerable and made us gag until I was nearly sick and Tahnee heaved.

A couple of weeks ago it would have been so bright in there you'd've had to squint to stop from going blind and jammed your fingers in your ears to shut out the bad 80s songs being piped through the store, but now it was dark and quiet as a cave. The shapes of the aisle shelves loomed up black in the gloom and boxes and cartons of goods were strewn about the place like fallen stones after an earthquake.

"Give me a torch Talon," she said, stiffly. "I'd rather find these myself if you don't mind."

Actually I couldn't have given a stuff, but I handed her

the smaller torch and watched as she switched it on and flashed it about the ceiling for a moment, reading the signs above the aisles. The light was a bit feeble even now and I remembered we had to get more batteries so leaving her to find her tampons I cut right and went off in search of the other shit we needed. Just for the hell of it I grabbed a trolley and the very act of that made me think of *Dawn of the Dead* when the two militia guys were checking out the shopping mall.

I never thought that I'd ever be living through something that seemed so much like a movie, but this was it. Using the feeble glow of the Maglite I started down the canned food aisle, surrounded by the silent gloom and the suffocating stink of rotting food. Cockroaches the size of mice scuttled off into the darkness as the light fell on the floor and shelves. There was a display halfway down laden with torch batteries so I dumped the whole thing in the trolley and started to head back.

Just then there was a shot. I dropped everything, found my gun in less than a heartbeat and shouted for the kid. She answered me from a hundred miles away and we made for each other through the gloom, tripping over things and stumbling in the darkness. I looked out towards the car park and saw nothing but a mangy dog running like hell on the far side of the street.

We met just inside the doors, crouching on each side.

Tahnee was shaking and holding the gun up at a dangerous angle so that if it had gone off it would have blown her face away. I reached across gently and pushed it down toward the floor, holding my own gun up to my lips as I scanned the car park, cursing myself under my breath. If anyone was out there, they would have heard us shouting.

There was nobody around.

Then Tahnee went white and I followed her gaze past me and to the left of the door. Carefully, I craned my head around and saw the drunk slumped on the ground. Most of his head was gone. In his left hand was a large pistol. I relaxed at once. Tahnee threw up.

I sat her down a little way from the doors to let her recover while I went back amongst the chaos and dug out a few other things we could use, then I raided the cigarette bar for the most recently-dated cartons and grabbed some rolling tobacco and a few packets of papers. Tearing open a packet of ready-mades, I lit one. Then I gathered up everything and shuffled Tahnee outside, looking around to make sure our dead mate's brain surgery hadn't attracted any attention. She set to work rearranging all our baggage to make room for the supplies and I took the guy's gun out of his hand. For some stupid reason I replaced it with my half-smoked Winfield.

I wonder if the anti-smoking lobby had ever thought of

doing something similar for one of their ads: Cigarettes Can Cause Your Head to Explode.

It was just after that we ran into Heckyll and Jeckyll.

Tahnee and I had talked a lot through the night. Without the noise of the bikes everything around us had been way too quiet and we'd obviously chatted to keep the ghosts away. By now though we were both feeling pretty fucked, and not in much of a mood for talking. All we both wanted to do was hit the hay.

So I guess we should have heard these two dudes coming, but in truth our defences were way down. If they'd been nasty, I guess we'd both be dead now, or I would be, at the very least.

I wear the shotgun across my back, King's handguns on each hip, I've got two knives on my belt and the single shot inside my boot. But I knew I would never have reached any of them in time if they had let that dog go. I've come up against Shepherds before and they're not fun enemies. As it was though, they were OK. There was a couple of tense moments when we all just stood there staring at each other with the dog growling low in his throat the whole time, but after a minute or so one of them just asked for a smoke, and that was it. The taller guy said something to the dog and it backed off and sat down, but it never took its eyes off me. It was some well-trained animal. If there was still a threat standing there on that corner, it was me, and the dog knew it.

I gave the guy a smoke and lit it and then we did the introductions. The guy with the dog was Garry. He was tall and thin with a long, acne-scarred face and a thin, straggly goatee like Shaggy from *Scooby Doo*. His buddy Pete was shorter, near to my height, with a more substantial frame and long brown hair. His face was round and oafish looking but his eyes were bright. He took a long pull from the cigarette like it was the first one he'd had in days and smiled.

"Fuck, that's all right!" he said. "You guys hungry? We're on our way back to our place. If you wanna you can come down."

He said it like he was asking his mates over for a barbie. Garry broke out into a stupid-looking grin and I wondered if that's exactly what we had been invited to, and whether that meant we were going to eat or be eaten. Nevertheless, we agreed and started walking with them down the dead and quiet street.

"You guys been walking all night?" Pete asked.

I nodded.

"Headed west, yeah? We'll probably head that way too eventually. Seen a few going that way in the last few days. Normally we try to avoid them, but looks like we didn't have much choice today, huh?" He grinned. "If you want and the others agree you can hole up for a while. We got a good little set up that'll keep us going for a while. Me and Garry were just out for a scrounge. Usually head out just before dawn for an hour or so, see what we can find and get back before anyone else decides to show up. Thought we heard a shot before. Was that you?"

With a bitter laugh I told them about the supermarket. Pete nodded silently.

"Wonder how many others have done that?" Garry remarked, and we all seemed to think about that for a minute or so. Nobody said anything and we walked to the end of the street and then left.

Two down from the corner on the opposite side of the road was a large double brick two-storey place. The windows on the bottom floor were bricked over and the portico was a minefield of broken bottles and coils of barbed wire. One of the large double garage doors was sealed shut with some heavy gauge concrete formwork that had been bolted securely to the archway. Pieces of masonry, sheets of fencing iron and rolls of barbed wire had been used in conjunction with the fence to construct a stockade around the property. The place was in what would have in earlier days been a quiet and out-of-the-way street that ended in a culvert with a narrow pedestrian bridge across it. To anyone who had bothered to come this way, it would have otherwise looked like just another abandoned relic of a previous time, but the way this one had been fortified it stood out like dog's balls. If a group like ours had found it, we would have attacked it at once and taken the place in a few minutes, if that.

But at least they were trying.

The balcony above the garage had been barricaded the same way as the perimeter. As we crossed the road, a skinny chick wearing sunglasses and a yellow bikini top peered over the makeshift parapet. Why she was wearing sunglasses when it was so bloody dark is beyond me.

"Who's that with you?" she challenged.

"Just a couple of lost souls heading west," Pete replied. "I told them if it was okay with everyone they could rest up for a while."

"Well wait there while I get Darren!" she shouted back and disappeared for a brief moment. Some guard, I thought, but going to get Darren obviously entailed shouting for him from just outside the door because we heard her doing exactly that and then she reappeared. After a few seconds, a shirtless guy with a big tattoo came out, followed by another chick with long, very dark brown hair. The three of them stood there for some time, sizing us up.

I wondered what they were thinking as they looked at us, a scruffy bikie dude in leathers and a top hat, armed to the teeth with a big crucifix around his neck, and a pretty young girl with short blond curls wearing navy cargo pants and a Northlane t-shirt.

After a minute or so, Darren told Garry to take the dog around the back. Then he moved forward and called down to Tahnee and I. The dark-haired girl stepped up next to him and I noticed with an inward smile that she was idly training a rifle on us. By the casual way she was handling it, I figured I could have drawn a gun, flamboyantly spun it around my finger like Indiana Jones and shot her before she worked out where the trigger was.

As it happened, I was wrong about that.

"It's okay to bring them up," Darren said. "But take the guns off him first."

As he said that, the girl with the rifle brought it to bear properly and aimed it, and I heard a click. I put my hands out and up and let Pete relieve me of the weapons. He didn't take the knives and didn't bother checking Tahnee at all, but it was clear that they had a distinct advantage.

Intelligently, Pete tossed them all into the backpack he had. Also quite intelligently, he kept hold of the shotgun.

"Let's go," he said cheerfully when he was done.

Garry had taken the Shepherd through a gate in the wall next to the house, and I thought we would go that way too, but instead the chick in the yellow bikini threw down a chain ladder that looked like it had been salvaged from a kid's playground.

Tahnee and I looked at each other and she raised an eyebrow.

Encumbered by the shotgun, Pete scrambled up with a little difficulty.

"What about our stuff?" Tahnee said to Darren. There was no way known we were going to get all of our shit up that ladder.

"Just leave it there for now. We'll send someone out to get it once we decide if you can stay or not."

"Well?" I said to Tahnee. She shrugged and meaningfully, but casually, patted her pants leg pocket. I pointed to my boot to let her know I still had a weapon too.

She started to climb.

Once we got to the balcony, Darren and the girl with the rifle shuffled us inside through a pair of sliding glass doors. The room beyond the doors was quite large and something of a shambles, but not too different from the sort of mess that a group of young people sharing a place would normally make, end of the world or not. One half of the room was taken up by a pool table and a bar. The other half was furnished with a wooden cabinet with glass doors that was full of videos and CDs, and an adjacent entertainment unit with a huge TV in it bracketed by a pair of massive stereo speakers hooked up to a DVD unit. Around the walls was an array of sofas of different styles and the floor was a mess of rugs, pillows, cushions, doonas and sleeping bags. Posters of grunge, punk and metal bands and fantasy artwork covered the walls like patchwork wallpaper. A big black square coffee table had been pushed over to one side of the room to allow space for whoever was using the floor as a bed. It was kind of amusing and a little surreal to notice that the table was crowded with beer cans, dirty ashtrays and pot paraphernalia. A large black ceramic bong rose up out of the clutter like a phallus.

Tahnee and I sat down on a sagging cane sofa that creaked loudly and wobbled when I settled my weight on it. I don't weigh a hell of a lot, so I'm guessing that chair was on its way to the scrap heap. It managed to hold, though and I broke out my smokes and offered them around. Darren, Pete and the dark-haired chick each took one and in return the girl went off and came back after a minute with some beers. Tahnee and I accepted them thankfully.

Darren dropped down in a battered leather sofa next to us and took a long haul on his smoke. He was a tough and wiry character with a colourful Chinese dragon tattoo that went from his right breast up over his shoulder and coiled along his spine. The dark-haired beauty sat down very close beside him.

"Darren James," he offered, and stuck out his hand. We

shook. "This is Michelle. I see you've met Pete and Garry already. That's Nicole out on the balcony; Steve and Kath are still out, but they're due back soon. Once they get here we can work out whether you can stay."

I nodded. "I'm Talon and this is Tahnee. Thanks for the beer."

"No probs." He flicked the ash off his smoke. "Garry's bringing your stuff up now. You guys want something to eat?"

Tahnee's eyes lit up and she almost leapt out of her seat in response. Darren chuckled. He patted Michelle on the thigh.

"Go and rustle up something for the visitors can you babe?" he said, and gave her a quick peck on the lips. She flashed a smile at me as she rose and went off to whatever part of the house the kitchen was at.

Before she got back there was a sharp whistle from outside and a minute or so later a nuggetty-looking guy wearing a Blood Duster t-shirt entered the room. Right behind him was another brunette, shorter and fuller-figured than Michelle and with hair a few shades lighter. At the same time, Garry came up the stairs and piled all of our gear on the pool table with the guns. A minute or so before, a noise that was unmistakeably that of a generator had started up from somewhere at the back of the place.

To my amazement, I recognised the newcomer. We'd

bumped into each other now and then in different offices when we'd been freelancing.

"Don't I know you?" I said stupidly.

"You do if you're Talon Willis," he replied amicably. "I'm Steve Davison. I used to work for *Street Machine*. Fancy meeting you here. Do you know who this is?" He prodded Darren just below the ribs. "This is Talon Willis! He writes for *Playboy*, *Street Bike*, *People*. Well, at least he used to! Fuck man I thought you'd be in gaol by now. Probably just as well you weren't huh? Unless you were smashed on prison moonshine and got over the wall once all the screws started dropping off the twig?"

"No, nothing like that," I said, the implication of what he had just said not lost on me. I would have made something of it, but just then the dark-haired hottie came back with some food. I had to look twice to make sure I was seeing it right, because what she brought in was a big bowl of garden salad and some baked chicken. Tahnee's eyes were on stalks.

"Where did you get all this?" she said, awestruck.

"The salad we grew," Michelle answered.

"And the chook we slew!" Steve added with a laugh. "The wogs down the road had a chicken run. We figured they wouldn't be using it anymore, so now we have one."

I guess I might have chuckled, but I was already eating

by then. Tahnee and I did everything we could not to wolf it down, but we couldn't help ourselves. After living out of tins for more than a week, this was like manna from heaven. Better!

By the time I had pushed my plate away, Tahnee had already finished and was curling up half asleep with a satisfied smile on her face. She linked her arm through mine and dropped her head on my shoulder.

It was the first sign of genuine affection she had ever shown me, and for a moment I was quite stunned.

Michelle went and got more beer and Darren stood up and dragged the coffee table closer to us.

"Wanna cone?" Steve asked, and plucked the bong from the centre of the mess.

For the first time in years, I actually said no. They seemed like an okay crowd, but we were living in desperate times and there was no way of knowing yet what they were capable of doing. The world had gone belly up more than a week ago and these people were living more or less like nothing had happened. That meant they were well stocked and well supplied, but just how they had come to be that way I still didn't know, and wondered how many others in the last few days had been invited back here for cones and beer and ended up with their throats cut for their trouble.

So instead of the dope, I fished out the zip lock bag in my breast pocket that had the very last of Doc's speed supply in it. I shook the bag in front of Tahnee, but she waved it away.

"I just wanna sleep," she mumbled, and that was fair enough.

I expected one of the others to ask for some, but no one did. I finished my beer, then another, and for the best part of the morning, we all sat and chatted as the bong went around.

I have to admit it was strange, like I'd stepped into another time when everything was just as it had always been. There was drugs, booze, women. One of the guys got up after a few minutes and put some music on that I didn't recognise. It was driving and explosive heavy metal with some nifty guitar work. Steve caught me tapping my foot idly to a rather catchy riff.

"You like this?" he asked, blowing a massive plume of pot smoke up to the ceiling.

"Yeah it's all right," I admitted. "I don't listen to metal much these days, but this is pretty cool."

"This is us," he said. "We just recorded this a month ago. The fucking album launch was supposed to be this weekend."

He laughed, then reached down under the table for something. After a moment he frisbeed a recent copy of *The Music* into my lap. It was open to a page featuring a quarter-size ad for a gig by a band called Terminus Est.

"Guess we could still play it, but we wouldn't get much of a crowd!"

After a couple of hours, the girls brought in some more food and we all ate. Tahnee was asleep on my shoulder, and the speed was wearing off so I knew I wasn't far off snooze time myself. I figured it was worth the risk. After all, they could have shot me when I first arrived. I kicked my boots off and stretched out on the rickety sofa after I'd set Tahnee down on one of the others. I was dimly aware of Steve and the rest moving around and talking but in no time I was asleep.

When I woke up it was late afternoon. Tahnee had woken before me and was sitting cross legged in the other half of the room listening to Darren and Michelle accompanying each other on acoustic guitars. There didn't seem to be anyone else around, but as soon as I moved the skinny chick called Nicole appeared out of nowhere and virtually gushed that she wanted to give me the guided tour. I went with her across the room. Tahnee gave me a little wave and a smile that was almost identical to the one Nicole had given me seconds before. It was the sort of smile you wanted to get from a woman, and it was beginning to look like an interesting evening.

I went down the stairs and out into the back garden with Nicole. We passed by the doorway to the garage and through the gloom I thought I could make out the shape of a two-door Falcon and what looked like either a Trans Am or a Stingray. Under the smog it was very dark; nevertheless it wasn't quite night yet and I could see well enough to nod or grunt as she pointed out the facilities. The house had been built on a large block that could easily have accommodated two such places. As it was, the area directly behind the house was taken up with a swimming pool and a barbecue area. Beyond that was a long, grassy yard inhabited by a couple of tin sheds, a large petrol-driven power generator mounted on the back of a truck, what I took to be a chook house further back in the gloom and, so Nicole told me, a vegetable garden and kennels for the dogs. I asked her how they'd managed to fit the generator truck into the yard and she casually explained that Darren and Garry had pinched it from a plant hire yard on the highway and driven it back. The others had hauled the fence down while it came in and then thrown it back up again. Luckily for them the fuel bowsers had still been working when they'd raided the place and so far they'd been running it six hours a day, mostly to run the fridge as everything else tended to be optional. The two-way radio set the group had ran on car batteries, they used hurricane lamps and candles for light, gas stoves for cooking and the impressive looking entertainment system was mostly for show. The CD I'd heard before had been played on a battery-operated Walkman-type pumped through a set of beefy computer speakers with built-in amplifiers.

"We don't really need that much juice," the skinny girl explained. "We run it for a few hours until the fridge starts to ice up, then we shut it off. A couple of times we leave it on for a while longer when the guys are using the Playstation, but it's too noisy and thirsty to have on all the time."

I agreed. I wondered silently how much longer they would be able to get away with running the thing before somebody or a group of somebodies heard it and came to investigate, and I found myself hoping it was going to be a long, long time. This was a good crowd, and they had few brains between them, although I'm pretty sure leaving a generator running so you could play video games in this sort of environment isn't a real clever idea.

If they could keep their chooks and their vegies going under all this smoke, they had a good chance of keeping it going once the smoke finally cleared. If it ever did.

We both stood there for some time not speaking, then she took me by the hand and led me back into the house.

Darren was still playing when Nicole and I got back inside, but Michelle had gone and Steve had taken over. For a brief moment I thought it was one of their own songs, but after a second I recognised it as an ancient Blue Öyster Cult track about a drug-related murder called "Then Came the Last Days of May." As I crossed to sit back down at the mess-ridden coffee table, Steve glanced at me pointedly.

"…They're OK, the last days of *man*," he sang, but it didn't seem like he meant it as a bad joke. It was more like bitter resignation, with a look of fatal inevitability. Whatever the rest of the might have thought about the situation, Steve Davison knew it was grim, bleak and without much hope. Even nestled as they were in their little early-twenties utopia of endless days and nights of indulgence with nothing to do but drink, fuck and take drugs, it was clear at least to one of them that the end was nigh.

Later, he and I went for a walk along the deserted streets around the house; ostensibly we went looking for construction material for continued shoring up of their place, but I knew it was merely an excuse for him to get away and talk.

We walked for about a kilometre just chatting idly about not much at all. After a few minutes he asked me how we'd fared on our little adventure so far and I gave him a bit of a run down. He was quite impressed by the account of my handiwork at the gun store.

"Sounds like you helped give this mess a bit of a hurry-on," he remarked after a low whistle. He grinned.

"Course it would have all gone up eventually. I saw the fire from the plane crash at Kurnell from here. Probably the one at Concord as well. You haven't been out that way at all, have you?"

"Not Kurnell, no," I said. "But we got a fair bit of the shockwave at the clubhouse. The initial explosion wasn't as big as I thought it would be. If it had all gone up at once it probably would have levelled everything for miles around. I guess that's when we really knew something totally fucked-up was going down."

The pair of us reached an intersection where a small mixed business had been ram raided by a black four wheel drive. The stink of days-old rotten food drifted out from behind the shattered roller shutter. A rat almost as large as a cat appeared from the darkness within and rose up on its haunches as if giving us the finger. Steve kicked an empty can at it.

"We've been listening to the radios a lot," he said. "There's quite a lot of people around the place... all over the world. The big one's a shortwave. We can get stuff from just about anywhere on it. We don't transmit much ourselves in case there's anyone around with a scanner and less than honourable intentions. That's why we put the dummy antenna up in the house down the road too. We've been thinking about barricading it to make it look like our place. Maybe do a few others around the place too, but I'm guessing if someone wanted it badly enough they'd find us eventually."

He shrugged and opened his mouth to talk again, but then stopped and a brief look of pain and torment crossed his face. Then it was gone.

"You know what we heard?" he said, suddenly. "The first night after this shit happened? Screaming and panic... Some guy just saying 'Please, help us! Anybody!' over and over again, and in the background it sounded like people were being murdered. They were on a cruise liner somewhere in the Pacific, just steaming around and around in a circle. Something had jammed the helm, all the crew was dead and they were just going round in a circle in the middle of the ocean. And all we could do was sit there and listen to them go fucking insane and slaughter each other. If you think this is fucked up here, can you imagine what it must be like for those poor cunts? Stuck on a ship in the middle of the ocean, probably fucking drawing lots to see who was gonna get eaten next?"

His voice was dead and his face was blank as he said it.

"We've heard it every night, with less and less noise going on in the background. Then last night we didn't hear it anymore."

He looked at me for a second and then turned back to the street we were walking.

"We've heard other stuff too... Guys reading the Bible, some fucking nutcase talking about blacks and Jews like it was all their fault, other people just reading shit or singing, ranting and raving. Pretty soon all the repeaters will shut down and then we won't get shit, and I'll be happy with that. At first we were trying to find if there was any other groups out there like us and maybe we could help each other out somehow you know? But there's just fucking crazies left. I don't even know why we keep it on now."

He shook his head and we walked on in silence for a few minutes. I broke out my cigarettes and we both lit one and pulled heavily. As if we weren't breathing enough smoke as it was.

"Me and Darren have been talking," he went on after a while. "If this fucking smog doesn't clear off soon, we're going to. I'd fucking rather not, but we're choking under this shit and we won't get our crops to grow. Have you noticed how there's no insects around? Plants need insects, man. Insects and sunlight, and we got neither."

"I was wondering about that," I said. "Apart from the need for human contact in a world turned to shit, what's keeping you all together? None of you could know much about agriculture, at least not enough to keep seven mouths full and as much as there's safety in numbers and you got the place boarded up pretty good, you probably wouldn't last five minutes in a fire fight."

Steve nodded solemnly. He knew all of those things as

well as I did.

"We're still a band, man," he said, shrugging. "Terminus Est! Darren and I have been living this for nearly ten fucking years. And Shelly and Kath are part of it too, all the ups and downs. We've all been together since high school, jamming, writing songs, fucking around in cars. I don't know if you saw the Trans Am in the garage… Darren and I practically rebuilt that car. It took three years. And the whole time we were playing in bands together, trying to build the perfect line-up. Then Gary came along and it was like we'd found a long-lost brother or something. He might be a bit of a newcomer but he's part of us now, and besides I know Gary'll stick with us 'cause he's got sense. Pete I don't have the same faith in. I trust him, but he's more like an in-law man, or a stepdad. There's not the same bond with him as there is with the others. He's got savvy though. He knows which side of his bread the butter's on. Nicole I couldn't give a fuck about. If she decides to hitch up with you guys when you leave, I wouldn't be surprised or care less."

I told him I wouldn't take her as far as the corner and he nodded.

"Yeah, you're right," he said. "She's not even a very good fuck. If it wasn't for the fact that she does fuck and doesn't care when, with who or with how many at once, we probably wouldn't keep her around. At least

124

she keeps Gary and Pete happy when they're up for a bit, especially now there's not much else going."

"Probably a good thing," I agreed. "You wouldn't want them coming onto your woman."

"Mate, I wouldn't care that much as long as they asked first, but Darren would! He'd skitz, and that's not a good thing to see." He paused dramatically and it was obvious from his expression that what he'd said was quite true.

"Have you done the teenybopper over yet?" he asked after a moment.

"No actually," I replied. "Come close once or twice I'll admit, though it probably wouldn't have been much fun for her. But she's a good kid and right now she's the only friend I got. If she ever wanted a bit there'd be no stopping me, but I ain't gonna force it."

"Well mate, by the looks of the body language she's being giving off tonight, I reckon you won't have to wait much longer."

I grinned.

We turned back the way we had come, and for a while again we were both silent. Off in the far distance, something exploded with a sharp, faint crack and a low rumble, but it was too far away to even hint at what it could have been. The sound seemed to trigger some thought in Steve's mind, and he reflected again on the polluted air.

Laughing, he said, "When I was in high school, I wrote a song called 'Nuclear Winter.' I thought I was being pretty fucking clever. I didn't know what the fuck I was talking about!"

We had stopped by now, and were sitting in a bus shelter like two late night revellers waiting for a ride home that would never come. Steve drew on his cigarette so hard it seemed to burn almost all the way to the butt. He coughed sharply and a great plume of grey smoke exploded from his face.

"You know, I been thinking," he said, waving away the smoke, "what's it like in other parts of the world? I mean it wasn't 2am Monday morning everywhere when this shit started to go down. Most of the world it was Sunday. I reckon there'd have to have been a few more people out on the piss than there were here at the time."

Like his earlier remark about prison moonshine, this comment struck me. I'd been thinking about something similar for a while, about some kind of connection between alcohol and surviving the Plague (or whatever it was), but I'd said nothing about it to Tahnee. After our adventure at the Superdome, I'd mused on it briefly but I'd gone off to sleep so quickly that I hadn't had much time to mull it over. Now Steve seemed to be thinking along the same lines.

I called him on it, and he seemed surprised that I hadn't already thought of it.

"I have," I said. "But I haven't really discussed it with anyone, although Tahnee's probably thought of it too."

"Well it makes sense to me," Steve replied. "I mean, it's pretty obvious this comet had something to do with killing everyone. Sort of like *Day of the Triffids*, except without the triffids, and a real comet not some evil defense mechanism. We were all fine until that came by. If it weren't for all the smoke and shit, you could probably still see it. Anyway, we were rehearsing that night, and as always, after a good jam, we came back here and got shitfaced. It's lucky we were out of milk when I woke up the next day or we might not have known what was going on until late that night. I walked down to the shop we were just at. It was open but no one was there. I grabbed the milk anyway and left the money on the counter like I do there sometimes because the owners know us from one time when Darren and I bashed a guy trying to hold the place up."

I wasn't sure I need to hear his life story, but I let him ramble a bit. It was probably making him feel better, and I could sympathise with that. At the same time, he must have realised that he was making a short story long.

"Anyway, when I left the shop I saw the smoke from the explosion at Kurnell, so when I got home I turned on the TV. After that, I got online, but that was a mistake. Conspiracy theory Heaven, that was. I'd hate

127

to see what it was like now. If it was still possible to get online that is. We started battening things down right away and trying to ring people we knew to see if they were ok. None of them were. We couldn't figure out why we'd been spared. It certainly wasn't the gods of heavy metal or anything stupidly Manowar like that looking after us. So we figured it must have had something to do with being rat-arsed."

I had to admit that it sounded pretty fucking stupid to me, but it also makes sense.

The night before the Plague hit, the boys and I had a bit of a meeting about dividing up some drug money and then we went on a bender. Dusty and Puller left early, and the next day, when everyone started dropping off the twig, only Dusty and Puller snuffed it. The rest of us were fine. Ordinarily that would be too small a control group to be drawing a conclusion like that, and I would have originally passed on it myself except that I remembered what Tahnee wrote. She was blind that night too. So was her friend Kelly. They cut school the next day because they were hung over, but their other friend, the one who got sick and died, hadn't been drinking with them. And the greenies they met up with who pulled off that stupid stunt at the zoo that got them all killed… well, if I remember rightly Tahnee said they told her they'd been on the piss for days. And now there's Steve telling me that he and his mates were righteously smashed as any good metal band should be after a hard night's rehearsing, so if you ask me, there's something in this little theory. Maybe this alien virus, if that's what it was, had a low tolerance to alcohol. Maybe alcohol in the bloodstream warded it off, or neutralised it in some way.

Well, whatever. For decades we've all heard the portents of doom from tee-totalling priests and temperance-minded conservative idiots, telling us about the hazards of the demon drink; advice columnists and doctors going on about moderation and abstinence like it was something to aspire to. And now look! The world's been left in the hands of binge-drinkers and booze hounds, derros and barflies and embittered old bastards who've been using booze bottle bottoms as eyeglasses for God knows how many years. And it all happened on a Sunday night too, when the only people who could get really pissed were dole bludgers and reprobates like me and Terminus Est who either didn't have to go to work the next day or simply couldn't be fucked.

We all might as well have just stayed up in the trees sucking back fermented coconut milk and picking nits for all the good evolving's done us. All that's left are vast wastelands of broken masonry and glass and useless metal and a bunch of brain-damaged yobs who probably can't even function properly now there's no beer around anymore.

"I wonder how much booze you needed in your system to neutralise whatever it was?" I mused. "A glass? A bottle? A mouthful?"

"Well let's hope it took more than a mouthful," Steve said, "or there's gonna be a fuckload of Catholics still alive in some time zone somewhere!"

We both laughed grimly at that prospect, and it occurred to me again that there probably was a few religious head cases about, looking up at the clouds waiting for Christ and the angelic horde to descend and whisk them up, alive, to Heaven. I wondered aloud whether clinging to forlorn hope was a good thing or bad.

"That's all we've ever had to cling to," Steve remarked. "Hope. Hope that things get better when they're bad, hope they can find a cure for the cancer you've got before it kills you, hope that when you do die, it's not just the end after all. You know, I think if it came down to roasting in Hell for a million eternities or simply ceasing to exist, most people would rather roast. The thought of complete annihilation is probably the scariest of all."

Being godless myself, I knew exactly what having that thought was like, and as it crossed my mind again then I was reminded of it quite forcefully. When I looked across at Steve, it was like looking into a mirror. Then he suddenly laughed and stood up.

"You know something Talon? Whether the world gets back on its feet or not, in ten thousand years, no one's going to know any of this ever happened!"

I nodded in morbid agreement.

"Kind of makes you wonder why we ever bothered at all, doesn't it?" I said.

"You bet. We're all just specks in the everlasting spectrum, never fully realising how insignificant we are. But I guess it's why guys like me want to go out and make records, in some futile hope that we'll be remembered for it one day."

I nodded again and flicked away my cigarette butt.

"I'm writing a book about all this, you know," I said.

"Yeah?" he replied with a bitter smile. "Who's gonna publish it?"

I returned his look.

"The same guy who's gonna put out your record!" I said, and we both laughed grimly and went back to the house, as empty-handed as we'd left.

I've spent most of today trying to stay away from Nicole. Late last night I woke up with the rather pleasant sensation of her lips around my cock. At first I thought – God, I hoped! -- it might have been Tahnee, but then I noticed she was still asleep beside me. Nicole had turned me onto my back and moved me away from her slightly. I didn't stop her from doing it of course and I even reached out and squeezed her little tits while she got me off. I dumped my load and she took it all like a twenty dollar whore. Then she giggled and tried to drag me away from Tahnee and wriggle up beside me, but I just grunted and shoved her off me. The bitch kept giggling for a couple of minutes like she was sucking back nitrous, trying to get me to fuck her, but I couldn't be bothered. I'd already shot my bolt. After a couple of minutes of her pawing at me and whispering "Come on, Talon," in my ear until I wanted to smash her face in, she finally slunk off into the darkness.

About a minute later I could hear her fucking someone else. Whether she was doing it to make me feel jealous or if it was just because she's a slut, I don't know or care. Anyway, the fucking tart's been following me around all day. It's not making Tahnee too happy and it's downright pissing me off. I don't know which one of the blokes here has a claim on her but if she was mine I'd be slapping her down.

I guess that's partly why I'm moving on, but mainly it's because I just don't want to be in this dead city anymore, even if it is in a drugs, booze and sluts paradise.

Things must be fucking bad if I'm giving up unlimited pussy!

Wednesday, September 12

[This first paragraph crossed out, but still legible]
Nicole's a scrag. I fucking hate that slut. I just know that last night she either fucked Talon or sucked his dick or maybe both. I'm gonna fucking kill her. Fuck her. And fuck him too. Why does he want to fuck her and not me? I bet he's never fucked a virgin before. Well pretty soon he will and then he won't want that slut anymore.

We left Steve and Kathy and the others as soon as it got dark. They came down with us until we got to the highway, except Pete and Nicole. They gave us some tomatoes and some eggs and some other stuff they said they could spare which was cool because now we're up the mountains there's not much around and most things would be pretty rotten by now anyway. Darren gave Talon some more speed too. I don't know where it came from but we had some and it was pretty good. I wish I was old enough to have seen their band play because I reckon they would be cool.

We said goodbye and started walking and after a little while we got onto the mountain road. There was still a few crashed cars and things around, but not as many as before. It was hard for the first few miles because it's pretty steep and it seemed to take ages before it levelled out a bit. But it was good because the smog thinned out a lot as we got higher up and just before we got where we are now we started to be able to see the stars again. We haven't gone real far up into the mountains, but Talon said we should stop and rest for a while which is cool because it's all been uphill of course and we're both a bit puffed out. We're sitting inside this building that used to be an information kiosk and we're both writing in our books. Earlier, Talon went down across the road to this little settler's cottage that the service station uses as a storeroom to see what he could find but there was nothing left.

I think Talon's a really good writer. He showed me some of what he wrote from before he met me. He won't let me read the rest, but he let me read the first few pages when we were on the way to Steve and Kathy's house. So I know about the big shoot-out he had and how all his friends died. I feel a bit sorry for him because of that. He's actually a really cool guy. I think I love him a bit. He's a tough guy but he's been good to me mostly except for the one fight we had. I scribbled out some stuff I wrote earlier where I said I was going to let him fuck me. I think I was just really jealous because of what Nicole and him did last night but if he asked me to fuck him I think I would. Hehe. I hope he doesn't read that part!

Thursday, September 13

We've walked pretty far since we left Kathy and the others. Like I wrote last night we walked up the highway to Glenbrook and stopped for a while to eat and then we walked through the National Park pretty much until nearly dawn. What was good too is that it rained finally. Me and Talon got totally soaked but we didn't care even though it was a bit cold. I was still wet and cold when we finally stopped walking but I was so tired that I just fell asleep straight away. When I woke up it was late in the morning and Talon was cooking. He made some fried tomatoes which I never used to like but beggars can't be choosers. They weren't too bad.

I like walking in the bush better than through the streets. I can breathe better and it's like nothing bad ever happened. I can pretend that I'm just on a bushwalk with my dad. Or probably not my dad! Maybe my boyfriend if I had one. I guess Talon sort of is my boyfriend now, except he's heaps older than me. I don't actually know how old he is but he looks about 25 or even 30, maybe older. I don't care. Without him I would be dead now. He's setting up the cooking stuff now so I might go take a shower under the little waterfall over there. I don't care if he sees me nude either. I want him to. Heehee. I'm a naughty girl.

Sunday, September 16

It finally rained. Tahnee and I were about an hour out of Glenbrook when it started coming down and a few minutes later it was like we were swimming standing up. Fuck it was good though. If there were any sane people around, they would have thought the pair of us were nuts. There we were, laughing and dancing like we'd just dropped the world's best acid, prancing about in the pissing down rain. I don't know if any of it got down to Sydney at all, but Sydney is a city of the dead, so that hardly matters anymore.

We had decided for the sake of prudence to take the bush tracks instead of staying on the road, so after a bit of a breather in Glenbrook we turned off the highway and wound our way down through the back streets to the national park. It was no darker in the bush than it was on the highway considering there weren't any electric lights around anymore, and no less eerie. It was a different kind of eeriness, though. Walking through the bush, it was almost as if nothing had ever happened to the world, like we were the only people who did and had ever existed. After the claustrophobic Sydney smog we were almost choked and smothered to death by the freshness and purity of the air and, after the rain clouds had finally snailed their way eastwards, dazzled by the stark clarity of the sky. The starlight seemed so bright it almost hurt. We heard other living things: night birds, insects (Steve had been right about that), frogs. By the time we stopped to sleep a little before dawn, I'd almost forgotten all the shit we'd been through in the past two weeks.

About midday we woke and polished off some fried eggs and tomatoes as a kick-start. The trail followed the course of a mountain stream that we used to freshen up and then we hiked for three solid hours before we stopped again. We talked a great deal, more than we ever had before. I guess we simply felt less paranoid that we would get jumped by thugs at every street corner, but it also could have been that whereas before we were oppressed by darkness and the rising stench of death, now we felt oppressed by the virtual silence. While we had escaped the Armageddon of the dying city practically unscathed, with the exception of our unfortunate experience in Homebush, we had rarely been out of earshot of muffled and distant explosions and occasional bursts of faint gunfire. On the forested trails of the national park, the only sounds were natural: the soughing of breeze through the leaves, the gurgle of a running stream, the chime of a bellbird or a whipbird cracking, crickets and frogs calling.

It was early that night that Tahnee let me take her virginity. I was unpacking the cooking gear and looking for a spot to set it and she had gone off under a small waterfall to take a shower. After a couple of minutes, she called me and I stumbled down in the semi-darkness to the place she was bathing. The moon was already up and the scene looked like a fairy grotto, a small, shallow pool under a cascade ringed by ferns, with little rainbows dancing everywhere. At first I couldn't see her, and then she stepped out from under the overhang that supported the waterfall. She was completely naked and nothing short of delectable in the moonlight. She made no attempt to cover herself, and from the look in her eyes, that was the last thing she was thinking of. Tahnee came slowly toward me like a water-nymph luring Hylas to his destiny.

As she drew close, she held out both arms. I reached for her, took one of her small, soft hands, then slipped on the wet stream bank and landed on my arse. She fell onto me of course and her light, wet, tight little body clung to me with her lips searching eagerly for mine. I rose, with her wrapped around me, and headed back up the bank, peeling off clothes and tasting her sweet young form as I did so. We climbed back to our campsite and I lay her down on the blanket. She gave out some breathless sighs as I sucked her tits into my mouth and slid a hand down to her thighs to part her. She was warm and wet, probably not wet enough for the first time but there was no stopping me now.

Until I began to push inside, I still wasn't sure if she was a virgin or not. When I felt how tight and tense she was, I knew for sure. She stiffened under me and gasped, then I felt her tear and she let out a sharp sob and tried for a second to pull away. I was too far gone to let her go now. She'd wanted me to fuck her, so she was going to get the full treatment. Her movements urged me on and I felt the tension in me snap and I blew. I followed through with a couple of heavy thrusts and then I dragged myself to one side.

Tahnee lie back for a moment panting deeply, in tears. I reached for her to let her know it was ok but she sprang away and scrambled off into the bracken, sobbing. I thought for a moment about going after her, but I didn't have the energy for it. Either she'd be all right, or I'd wake up in the morning alone. It probably felt like rape to her, I guess, but that was just how sex is with me.

I slept pretty soundly that night; the next morning I was surprised to find her curled up against my chest under the tangle of blankets. I kissed her forehead and shifted her gently, then got up and went down to the creek to wash up. I didn't even bother throwing my strides on and when I looked around from the waterfall a few minutes later I noticed that Tahnee hadn't bothered either. She grinned mischievously when she saw me rise, stepped close and patted me. I guess she must have got something out of the previous night after all.

The next thing we were at it again, under the cascade, fresh mountain spring water dancing over our bodies as we fucked in a fern-rimmed forest pool like some romantic erotic fantasy come true. I tried to be more gentle this time, and I lasted a lot longer before I came and fell away from her onto the bank.

We spent that day under the canopy of leaves, thoughts of pressing ahead far from our minds. Neither of us was in a mind to even dress. Why did we need to? The weather was mild and we were completely alone and perfectly at ease for the first time in many long, long days. Who was likely to find us out here, in a world where not enough people were left alive to make a decent football crowd anymore? I even toyed with the idea of simply staying where we were for good, or at least for more than a little while. Just living off the land and fucking. There was a decent overhang close by, plenty of fresh clean water and undoubtedly a good supply of fresh food free for the taking. It could well be months, if ever, before anyone else was likely to come along the same route.

Of course, we're on the verges of what passes for civilization these days again now, so obviously we did move on, but for just that one day we lived like a pair of hippy flower children at one with nature. Just before sunset we fucked again and it was very late and very dark when we woke to find a misty rain touching everything like a fairy lover.

At first light, we reluctantly left our idyllic love nest. A light, early morning mountain fog clung to the ground, plunging the trail into a pleasant woodland gloom of pale greys and greens. We eventually had to leave the shelter of the scrub because the trails petered out and we crept carefully along the back streets of some mountain suburbs, but after a while we couldn't even do that anymore and we had to follow the highway along a narrow ridge and through a series of cuttings. At one point, we could look back east over the ruin of civilization. We stopped there briefly, but I only wanted to be off this stretch and be safe again in the bush so we hurried on without too much delay. Late in the afternoon, we reached the railway station at Woodford and Tahnee remembered a trail nearby that she'd taken with her dad once, and again I found myself wishing that I could have had her dad instead of mine. By nightfall we'd reached the bottom of a valley and camped next to a stream.

That was yesterday, and today we were off just after first light again. By noon we discovered the trail we had been hiking ended at what almost passed for a proper road, although in truth it seemed like not much more than a slightly wider fire trail that someone had decided needed a half-arsed going over with a grader and after another hour or so of climbing we emerged from the bush among the cottages of a mountain village. In a few minutes, the road we were on met another, rather more important looking one at a T-intersection. I knew that we were still on the south side of the main drag through the mountains, even if I didn't have a clue exactly where we were, so we took a few seconds to stop and think. I still wanted to stay away from the highway and avoid any human dregs that might still be on the move west or just sitting pretty somewhere like a spider waiting for a fly, but for the moment it didn't look like we had much choice as to where to go. At least if we got to the highway, I'd know more or less where we were, but as it happened we didn't have to go as far as that to find out.

Tahnee slipped two fingers through my belt loop as she stood beside me in the middle of the road. I reached out to slip my arm around her and then she spoke out.

"I think I know where we are!" she said. She grabbed my hand and pulled me along the street to the left of the one we had just left.

We walked up a slight rise toward another street. There was a black and white sign nailed to a pole there that said "Observatory".

"My dad brought me here a couple of times," she said, with a warm smile. "There's a really cool spot down here."

We turned down a street that led down a hill and back up again. Low, stunted heath-like vegetation was interspersed with some modest-looking homes. A fox appeared from a bush on the right, looked at us, and then slunk off back the way it had come. Close to the end of the street was a low brick house with an observatory dome behind it. A sign advertised that it would be open this weekend.

We passed it by, arriving at an unsealed road that ran left and right. Tahnee went left, and I followed. A hundred metres or so further down, there was a low, single rail gate on the right hand side. She stepped over it and walked out onto a flat, bald expanse of rock overhanging the cliff. It offered a truly spectacular, completely unbroken, 360 degree vista of the Jamison Valley and the tableland we were on, with Mount Solitary looming to the south and Narrow Neck disappearing into the distance to the west. A green, early afternoon haze swam above the trees below. I looked over the edge and saw the wrecks of some cars that had been dumped over the cliff, slowly rusting and being covered with greenery. Almost every square inch of the rock shelf we were standing on had been carved with initials and dates.

"What do you think?" Tahnee said suddenly. "It's pretty cool, huh?"

I had to admit that was something of an understatement, but the practical side of me was wondering how this spot could be of use to us apart from its unobstructed view of everything around. Then she answered my question.

"Come on," she said, as I was still looking around, and I saw her moving off through the scrub. I turned to follow her and she led down a rough trail under the shelf. From here, the rock above formed a high, shallow cave with a sandy floor. Someone or a group of someones had once been rather industrious here. An extremely low tunnel reached far back under the overhanging stone, dug out of the sand by busy hands. Across the cave mouth, a wall about a metre high had been built many years ago out of sandstone remnants. There was even the ruin of a fireplace or chimney, blackened with soot. It wasn't just thrown together either. Whoever had built this had even gone so far as rendering the outer wall. By the look of it, it might have stretched all the way to the roof once.

"Pretty cool, huh?" she said again, and I had to agree. You could actually live here for quite some time if the need arose and you were prepared. Without water and only a little food, we weren't prepared enough to stay for long, but it was certainly a good spot to rest for the remainder of the day at least.

We unloaded all our stuff and piled it into the tunnel at the back of the cave before climbing up again and heading back to the last few houses we'd past to scavenge what we could from them. On the way I had to shoot a huge cat that leapt out of some scrub into our path. Without needing to be asked and not showing any sign of repulsion that she may have a month or so ago, Tahnee stuffed the carcass into a tote bag. We entered the yard of the first place and cats scattered everywhere. I didn't bother wasting bullets trying to shoot one of them. They were too quick and the one we had would be enough for a good meal. The door wasn't hard to break down. There was no trace of any former resident, but all around the place was a strong smell of cat piss. I wasn't worried about cats as much as I was, and am still, about dogs, but the number of the mongrels I'd seen outside did urge caution.

Opening the fridge in the kitchen was like opening a tomb. The stench of meat that had rotted almost into a black mass and milk products that were almost able to get up and walk away assaulted both of us. It was so bad it made my eyes sting. Tahnee heaved violently and spewed. Nonetheless, there was an unopened bottle of Coke and two bottles of water with unbroken seals in the door shelves, so I grabbed those and we left.

Cats scattered again when we got outside. Unlike the one I'd killed, these ones were likely newly feral and still had some fear of man in them. Pretty soon, they'd fear nothing and no one.

When we got back to the cave, I scouted around a little to make sure there was only one way down to it and I set up a few tripwires around the place so that we'd be warned of anyone who might come snooping around. I skinned and gutted the cat while Tahnee gathered firewood and then we fucked while it cooked on a spit over the fire. It didn't taste too bad.

As the afternoon wore on, we talked a great deal, about old friends and family as if they were still alive and we'd see them all again when we got home. Tahnee talked a lot about her friends Kelly and Dara and all their goofing off and cutting school, and about all the cool shit she used to do with her dad. It was happy talk, but also tinged with sadness, yet I felt at ease. It put me to mind of the time my two oldest cousins took me to Canberra with them one weekend and we drove up to Mt Ainslie and set off fireworks until we got busted by cops. After that we went to Braddon and dragged a few guys. Later on James got half-tanked and tried to swim across Lake Burley Griffin with his clothes on but as soon as it got a little deep he went under and we had to fish him out.

We had a fucking blast that weekend. I told Tahnee the whole story before I realised I'd never really told anyone about it before, and I actually felt very pleased that I had finally done so.

As the sun set behind the mountains before us, carving out the cliffs dramatically like bas relief, we fucked again and as I went to sleep I found myself thinking that I kind've liked the new world I was in.

I couldn't have been asleep all that long when I heard a small truck. It sounded louder than God in the utter quiet but I must have been in a deeper sleep than usual because it was already quite close when it woke me. Tahnee was already awake. It was so dark I couldn't see her even though she only a foot or so away, but I knew she was awake because she urged me to shush. I figured that was kind of needless because the truck was so damn loud we could have been playing death metal at full volume and they wouldn't have heard us, but I shushed nevertheless. I scrabbled for my pants and a gun at the same time. There were a few reports that were either backfires or shots, then the motor cut. We both noticed a swath of light cut through the pitch dark like a lighthouse beacon, throwing up the walls of the valley in the distance as it passed above us. I crept outside and cut right along the ledge, trailing a finger on the wall. The starlight wasn't enough to show me how near to the cliff I was. Since the motor had cut, I'd heard doors slam and then nothing. To me, that could only mean whoever was coming thought someone might be here. After a minute or so, I heard someone shout from almost directly above me that it was all clear and a short time later the truck door slam again. But this time, only one door slammed. I didn't need to wonder why.

The truck started, turned and started driving away. It

didn't sound as loud as before, and hadn't gone far before I heard a thud followed quickly by the rattle of an empty tin and someone say "Fuck!" Torch beams exploded into being from about six directions. It was my turn to say "Fuck", but I did it silently.

"If someone's down there, you'd better come out," demanded a voice that sounded like a cop's. "We know someone was there before! We saw your fire. If you're still there, come on out!"

I crept forward again, to the gap in the wall that served as the door. I felt Tahnee's hand brush mine and I closed it in a fist. I slipped my gun into my belt at my back and with Tahnee in tow, I headed out. There was no other choice.

As we swung around and up on the narrow trail, we saw two dark figures looming ahead. They saw us too. A torch light hit us in the face from higher up on the left.

"Stop there," said the cop's voice. "Just the two of you?"

"No," I said. I hated voices like this guy's. "There's a whole fucking army in that cave. They're midgets, and I am their king."

Our visitors obviously didn't know how to respond to that.

"Very fucking funny," said cop voice after a few seconds. Someone evidently thought it was, because there was laughing further away to the left. "Come on up here, Your Majesty, and keep your hands in sight."

It was a dumb thing to say. Only an incredibly deranged psycho would have tried anything now.

We walked toward the two figures ahead. One of them asked, "Are you armed?"

"To the teeth," I replied.

They marched us up onto the rock and we stood there while they went down and brought up all our gear. The cop-sounding guy said nothing until everything had been piled up beside us. Someone finally realised I still had a gun stuffed down my pants, and removed it. As soon as it became apparent that we were no longer a threat, or as much of a threat that one man and a teenage girl could be to seven guys armed with automatic weapons, the guy in charge changed his tone, but not much. He was more polite, but made it aware that he was the Guy in Charge.

"How long have you two been here?" he asked.

"Since about midday," I said. "Things are a bit shitty down in Sydney so we thought we'd take a day-trip."

"You're a bit of a smart-arse, aren't you?"

"That would be an understatement."

I couldn't see his face in the dark, but I'll swear that his eyes narrowed. Then he asked for names, and we gave them.

"Can I put a shirt on now?" I said. "It's fucking cold here."

After a moment of silence, I added: "I swear I won't pull a gun out." I put my hand across my heart and gave a Cub Scout salute. Tahnee giggled.

To my surprise, the Guy in Charge grunted a half-laugh and stepped back.

"Be my guest," he said.

After that, they let us bundle up our stuff and walked us back toward the truck. By the time we got there, the mood was somewhat more relaxed. The Guy in Charge's name was Scott. He actually apologised for being a hard-arse and introduced his companions, although I only remember two of their names now. Clive was a bespectacled guy with close-cropped hair who looked like a portly accountant and had hands like dough and Pete was a rough-looking lad who I learned later had once been a first grade Rugby League player. Each time I looked at him he glanced away, pretending he wasn't perving on Tahnee's chest puppies.

The truck was a 3-ton flatbed with an enormous searchlight mounted on the roof next to a machine-gun. In a large cage behind the cab on the driver's side was a reasonably-sized pile of dog and cat carcasses, one dead roo and a deer.

As we drove past the place we'd raided earlier, I tapped Pete on the shoulder and said, "Have you been in there yet? It's like a livestock supply for a Chinese restaurant."

He laughed and said he'd be sure to come back and check it out.

The truck crawled loudly through the darkness, along a narrow road past scrub and dark empty houses and finally the looming shape of a water tower before heading west onto the highway. A few wrecked vehicles littered the roadsides but the main part of the road itself was clear. After a couple of kilometres, we came to a section that was partly blocked by the remains of a railway bridge and the truck turned off along another narrower road. Pete explained briefly that the bridge had been blown up on purpose to divert anyone who came along down this road instead. They'd blocked other roads too, with building rubble, trucks, trees and anything else they could find that wouldn't be passed through easily and if some of the others were to be believed there were booby traps and makeshift land mines all over the place. I wasn't sure if anything they could do would stop any group that was determined enough, yet I had to agree it would make life difficult. Others muttered their agreement, but so far they'd had no trouble.

We turned down the main street through Leura. Unsurprisingly, virtually every shop on both sides appeared to have been thoroughly ransacked. A few minutes later, the truck had crawled painfully up the hill, wound through a couple of tight turns and lurched into Katoomba. The grand old edifice of the Carrington Hotel sat back from the main road at the top of a grassy hill. The truck turned into the driveway and halted near the entrance. As it pulled up, more guys with guns came outside. Tahnee and I climbed down and Scott and Clive led us inside.

The one time I'd been to the Carrington before, it had looked more like a museum than a hotel. Now it looked like a museum that had been turned into a military base. Cables ran everywhere with lights hanging off them, crates and boxes were piled in corners and there were people walking in and out of rooms with walkie talkies and rifles. We followed Scott and Clive into a large room where floodlights had been set up in the corners and a huge sheet of butcher's paper with a hand drawn map of the town covered one wall. A tall guy wearing a police uniform and a woman in grey slacks and a pale green blouse were looking at the diagram as we came in. They both turned toward us.

"Ah, Scott, you're back," said the cop. "All clear?"

Scott nodded and took a step to one side.

"We found these two camped out on the Tableland at Little Switzerland," he explained. "They came up from Sydney for a bit of a look around."

"Did they?" The cop looked us over quickly. "Find anything interesting?"

"A few feral cats," I said. "They're not too bad spit-roasted."

A couple of weeks ago he probably wouldn't have thought twice about twisting my arm behind my back, snapping on a pair of cuffs and tossing me in a cell for a while, but now the old cop just chuckled. I took a moment to look he and his companion over. He was well into middle age and the dark brown hairs at the crown of his head were fighting a losing battle against the grey ones that surrounded them. While he was starting to go to flab, he stood straight and tall and I noticed he had gigantic hands and blotchy skin like an alcoholic. The woman was mid-forties and still quite good looking and in good shape although her features were a little angular and she quite obviously dyed her hair.

"Well I'm afraid you'll be eating a lot of them for a while to come unless a miracle happens," continued the cop. "Either that or dog. There isn't a lot of fresh meat to be had otherwise."

"So we noticed. Looks like you're not short on hardware though," I said. "I always thought Katoomba was a hippie town, not a haven for gun nuts."

"We're adaptable."

I had nothing to say to that. He started to say something else, but just then Pete and another guy came in with our gear and the woman directed them to put it off to one side.

The cop introduced himself as Robert Coleman and the woman as Heather Barry, and then Tahnee and I jumped through a few simple hoops for them: who we were, if we were "together", whether we knew of any others hiding out in the scrub somewhere. Then they asked if we wanted something to eat and, as it was likely we'd only get stewed cat or something, we passed it up. Heather took us off to one side and sat us down while she spoke to someone on a walkie talkie. A minute or so later a grey-haired old woman about a hundred years old came in. She had a doctor's bag in one hand that looked nearly as old as she was and almost the same size.

After giving the pair of us the briefest of examinations, she waddled away and we were told to grab our stuff and go with Clive to find our lodgings. I thought he'd take us somewhere in the hotel but as it turned out we walked a little way down the block and across the road to a church. A derelict was passed out on a bench outside. Clive paid no attention to him at all and took us in.

It was dimly lit by an array of hurricane lanterns and votive candles. A girl about nineteen wearing only a bra and a pair of shorts and a guy about the same age in a singlet and jeans were drinking bourbon and playing cards at a table. Several other young people were laying around on mattresses, smoking and drinking. They all looked around at us.

"I'll leave you to it," Clive said, quietly, and left. For some reason, he seemed uncomfortable in the place.

I left Tahnee to do any introductions while I took our gear and found a queen size mattress over by the chancel. I dumped the bags and crashed down on the mattress. No one objected, so I stretched out, found the baggie in my luggage that Steve gave me and rolled a joint. I took a couple of good pulls, crushed it out with my fingers and went to sleep.

It must be close to dawn now. Tahnee's curled up beside me. A couple of kids are trying to have a quiet fuck somewhere nearby. That's rather amusing considering this is a church. My mother would have a heart attack. I'm not sure how well things are being run here, but so far it looks like someone's at least trying to organise a little. I guess I'll find out more in a few hours.

Monday, September 17

I looked back at the first date in my book before and it's only been 13 days since the end of the world. It seems like heaps longer than that sometimes and others it seems like it all happened just yesterday.

We got to Katoomba last night after some guys in a truck picked us up. We were camping in this spot that dad took me to once and we ate a cat (yuck) and then when it got dark they all turned up and brought us here. Some cop and some lady that looks like a teacher are in charge I think. His name is Robert and hers is Heather. After we'd talked to them a fat dude took us to a church where we slept last night. There's a bunch of other people here with us. Most of them are a bit older than me, but I don't suppose too many kids my age would have lived through the Plague, except for those cunts at the stadium. I had a bad nightmare about that last night. I kept on waking up and then I found a joint in the bed that Talon had only smoked half of so I had some more and I slept ok after that.

Last night I met this girl Lauren and her boyfriend Drew. They let me drink with them and play cards for a while until Drew said we should play strip poker. After that I went and started talking to some of the others. I don't think I like Drew much. He's a fucking retard. There's three other girls called Toula (I think), Maria and Christine and five guys. One's called Sam and another one is Matt but I can't remember the others. They all seem ok I guess. They asked me a lot about Talon and what had happened to us before we got here and I told them stuff about how we met.

Today me and Talon went back to the hotel to learn a bit more about what was going on up here. While we were waiting to see Robert we had some breakfast in the dining room which is this huge old-fashioned room with big chandeliers and columns. It would have been a pretty posh place to have dinner before the Plague and it looked kind of funny with all the tables pushed up together down the middle of the room and bunches of people sitting around in dirty clothes eating baked beans. Most of the people here are locals but a few are like us and came up from the city as well as others who were from the other side of the mountains who had come this way trying to get to the city for help. Everyone looks sad and hungry. While we were sitting there just talking quietly to each other, a woman near us just started freaking out. She was screaming and then she started laughing and crying at the same time and then she just ran out of the room. People looked at her but no one followed her to see if she was ok. Then a bit later she came back like nothing was wrong and started eating again. I reckon I would have gone mental ages ago if I hadn't met Talon.

Anyway after breakfast we went to see Robert. He was sitting in a big leather armchair drinking brandy and talking to some of the dudes from last night. When he saw us he called us over and told us to sit down. The other guys went away and then he started explaining a few things. Robert said that for the moment there was plenty of food. They'd gone around to all the stores and shops and packed up everything that was in cans and jars and bottles and stored it all in the hotel which they'd turned into a headquarters. There is a vacant lot next to the hotel which they were making into a farm with chickens and goats and some cows that they'd rounded up from yards. There wasn't much fresh food except for cats and dogs and other ferals that the patrols shot but they were already planting vegies and things. There was heaps of medical supplies that they'd collected from the hospital and all of the chemists in town. The plumbing was still working mostly but he was worried about how long it would keep working for and how to fix it once it stopped. Everyone had been given different jobs and he said that he would have to find something for us to do. Talon volunteered to help out on the patrols and I asked if I could do something around the hotel. He asked what I could do and I said "Anything". Then he said he'd get Heather to show me around and give me a job.

Heather came in after a while and I went with her while Talon stayed and talked more with Robert. He hasn't said what they talked about yet but he looks a bit worried.

Anyway, they got me helping out with the sick, which is

cool because Lauren does that too and it's nice to have a girl to talk to again. There's a few sick people, not that many, but there's only two doctors and one of them is that really old lady who examined us when we first got here and she can't do much. She must be about 70 at least. I don't know what will happen if she dies because there's too much work for just the one guy who would be left. The first floor has been turned into a hospital area and there's about two people in each room. Me and Lauren spent the day feeding and nursing them. Mostly it's ok except when someone shits themselves. Even though I've seen a lot of dead bodies now, cleaning shit out of someone's arse is still pretty gross.

Talon came up for a while to get his burns looked at but they're mostly fine now. They weren't that bad in the first place, just like really bad sunburn.

After work me and Lauren went down to some creek to wash clothes. The water was pretty cold but I washed myself too. Then we sat around and had a few smokes and talked about things.

"I don't know how long I'm gonna stay here, Tahnee," she said. "I haven't said anything to Drew or the others but I don't know how long this place can last. There's fights all the time and people keep getting sick. Last week there was only three people sick and now there's a dozen. And no one knows how to do anything. If something breaks down there's only one or two guys who know how to fix each thing. It's gonna take ages for

159

everyone to learn everything we need to know to keep this place going."

"What are you going to do then?" I asked.

"I wanna go find somewhere and live by myself with one or two others to help out where it's just us looking after ourselves. It's nice to want to help everyone, but we can't. There's too many people here and not enough to go 'round for that long. When the farms start growing and things, maybe, but that'll take months and by then there won't be much food left and we've already hardly got any water. You know where I was thinking about? You can't tell anyone yet because I haven't said anything to anyone, ok?"

"OK," I said.

"I reckon somewhere like Jenolan Caves would be a good place to go. There's heaps of water there and they've even got a dam that runs a power plant. Bushrangers and stuff used to hide out there like over a hundred years ago. You could probably live there for ages."

"Probably. But don't you think other people might have thought that already? What if you went there and there was already heaps of people there?"

"I dunno. Just go somewhere else I guess until I found a place. But I know that it would be dumb to stay here much longer."

Maybe she's right. I don't know. But later on when Talon got back I talked to him about what she said and he seems to think she's right too. I know that he really doesn't want to stay here. That's ok. I'll go wherever he goes.

Thursday, September 20

I knew almost as soon as we got here that there wasn't a great deal of hope for this place. Robert and Heather and a few of the others are working reasonably hard at creating the illusion of a community here, but in reality it's more like one of those East African refugee camps they used to show on the news, except it's full of white people drinking Coke and carrying firearms. No one's quite starving yet but it's clear they will be soon. There are just too many people here and not enough resources. The sick are starting to outnumber the healthy. In the five days we've been here, the infirmary ward they set up at the Carrington has gone from crowded to full and with only one alcoholic sawbones and a near-blind septuagenarian to look after them all, it's going to be easier just to shoot some of them soon. There are other problems too. Yesterday a generator broke down and it took six guys three hours to fix it because the three mechanics we've got were out shooting dogs. The plumbing in most places still seems to work okay, but no one seems to know how long that will last. They've done planting and rounded up livestock to supplement the stores of food but it'll be months or a year before they've got enough to make a salad and no one will be left alive by then.

Of course, in theory this community could work. If everyone knuckled down, if the few with mechanical and engineering knowledge could teach a few more, if people were prepared to keep living hand-to-mouth and surviving on boiled water, baked beans and stewed dog. But that ain't gonna happen. Maybe if we'd all come from the Mongolian steppes or villages in Vietnam, we could keep this place going for years. Aborigines lived here for tens of thousands of years and they didn't even have agriculture. But these aren't people used to living in the Stone Age, or even the Dark Ages. Most of them are kids, or blokes like me who are used to turning on a tap to get water or flicking a switch for light without a second thought as to how it all happens. Two weeks ago we were living in a society where you only had to make a phone call to get a pizza delivered. The hardest thing we've ever had to do for a meal might have been to walk to the take-away for a kebab. Now we're all expected to hunt and farm and build things and work by candlelight, and GO WITHOUT – just like that? Not fucking likely. A few might be prepared to do that, but there are a few hundred people here. Sooner or later the supplies they have here are going to run out, and that's going to be long before they've grown enough of their own food to replace them. What then? No one's going to come along and help. If anyone does come, it will probably be to take whatever there is left to take, and from what I've seen of the "defences" this crowd have put up around their little haven here, it won't take much

163

of a raiding party to strip this place to the bone.

It's already starting to break down. Tonight there was a loud debate in the lounge about the number of people here. Since Tahnee and I arrived, there have been about twenty others who've drifted into town. Now there's a bit of a feeling that we shouldn't be taking in any more or that if we do, we only take in "useful" people like doctors or mechanics or someone who knows more about farming than just putting seeds in the ground and chucking water over them.

"What exactly do you suggest we tell people?" Robert demanded. "There's no more room at the inn?"

"Too fucking right," snarled one of the patrol group leaders, a sour bastard named Dan Mitchell. I'd been in Mitchell's group on my first night but only lasted that one trip because I'd almost bashed his face in within the first ten minutes. He's a useless, self-centred cocksucker who's never done a hard day's work in his life. Once upon a time he was in some dead-end public service middle management job where the only thing he'd ever done was throw his weight around and swear at people. "You can't sit around like Bob Hawke letting in useless strays without any skills! Look at that fucking gook bastard that turned up yesterday. He can barely speak English. What are we feeding cunts like him for when we can't even feed the people we've already got?"

"That 'gook bastard' happens to be an auto-electrician, Mitchell" said Scott. "In case you haven't noticed, we still have a few trucks and cars around the place that might need a guy like him. And if we're going to argue about keeping skill-less arseholes around, you haven't exactly contributed much outside of hot air and bullshit. You can't even keep a team together."

"Maybe if you'd give me a decent team instead of any bludger that blows in, I could keep things together."

"You couldn't keep things together with a roll of gaff and a nailgun, fuckhead," I said. He wouldn't meet my gaze.

"Another thing you might not have noticed Mitchell," Scott continued, "is that we don't have much of a choice as to who just blows in. In case you've forgotten, it's just about the end of the world! If you want to save what's left, you're going to have to do with what you've got "

Mitchell took a step back at that, and pushed out a long breath. Despite my opinion of him, I had to agree with what he said next.

"That's my whole point. I don't think it can be saved. I reckon we'd all be better off if we started to worry more about saving ourselves than trying to save a whole bunch of other people. The time for that sort of shit is over."

"So what do you suggest we do about all the people we

have here already? Cut them loose?"

It was Robert who asked.

"I'm not suggesting that," Mitchell said. "If you'd listened to what I said in the first place, I said we shouldn't let more people stay. We've probably got too many as it is, but I'm not gonna tell you that we should kick people out. I'm not an animal. We can barely look after the people we've got as it is."

"Mitchell's right," I said. "It's time to draw up the barricades. If you want to keep this place going for the people who are here, you can't keep letting more in. I know it sounds heartless, but there aren't the resources here to keep expanding the population or it's going to end up like some tent city in the Sudan. There's plenty of other towns around. Let them hole up there. And I'll tell you what else. You'll never be able to defend this place with the huge perimeter you have around it. A few piles of rubble across the highway won't stop anybody. You need to seal off this part of town and concentrate the defence in this area. I'm surprised you haven't thought of that before."

"It's been discussed," Robert said.

"You better do more than discuss it. You can guarantee that mine wasn't the only club that lived through the plague, or the only group like it. There must have been thousands of people who survived at first. There was a footy final on the night before remember. If being drunk was the reason we managed to live through the night, then there would have been a lot of shitfaced people stumbling around the next morning and not all of them would have been hopeless retards. I daresay some of them would have been servicemen, cops and others who know how to fight and survive. The day after it all started we ran into a group of Lebs armed to the teeth and it was only pure luck that I got out of that little tussle in one piece. No one else did. Once any of the gangs that are still left in the city stop killing each other, you can be sure that whoever's left won't stay in Sydney forever. It's over down there. You might get one really strong band that'll take over whatever there is left and stay put, but any others will get forced out or just go looking for somewhere else to loot. Sooner or later some of them might come this way, and when they do, they'll do it with guns blazing. There might not be a helluva lot of ammunition left to go 'round by the time they start sniffing at the walls of this place, but don't think they won't put up a fight. And it won't be pretty."

It was obvious from the reaction that this had been talked about before, but that no one had come up with a really good plan to combat the problem. I found it interesting that even the guys who had Army and Police training had done virtually nothing to properly fortify the town and very little in the way of organising things properly. It was almost as if they'd decided to try and get the place up and running first and worry about defending it later.

"It's time we had another meeting," Mitchell suggested. "This time, get everyone here and don't bullshit to them. They need to be told how things are, and how things are gonna be, and if they don't like it, they can leave."

"That would include you too, I take it," said Scott.

"I'll be fucked if I'm going to leave. I've done too much work to get this place up and running to take off somewhere else and start again."

"You might not be left with any choice," Scott threatened.

"Oh really? Just what the fuck is that supposed to mean?"

I stood up then. Mitchell had a semi-automatic and there was no telling how far he might go. I certainly wasn't going to wait for him to start a massacre.

"Looks like the ball's in your court Coleman," I said to Robert. "If you're supposed to be in charge here, you better do something to restore some order. It's pretty obvious things aren't going to plan, so you better come up with a better plan. As much as I think Mitchell's a piece of shit, he's got a point. This isn't a council you're running with a bunch of wannabe politicians arguing about fixing potholes. This is a refugee camp that could turn into a war zone at any moment. I've been here for a few days and there doesn't seem to be anyone doing much except for a bunch of blokes traipsing about with guns and walkie-talkies like wog security guards in a shopping centre. There's a derro sleeping on the bench outside the church. What good is it keeping wastes like that around the place?"

Coleman put his hands up.

"OK," he said. "OK, you've got a point. Let's call a full meeting for tomorrow morning. Make sure everyone turns up. Let's try and curb our aggro until then, shall we?"

"No guns," Scott suggested.

"Yes, good idea. In fact, from now on, everyone checks their weapons at the door here unless they're on duty here."

Things are quiet now. When I got back here to the church I told everyone about the meeting tomorrow. Most of them were pretty indifferent about the news. Tahnee and Lauren were quite interested however, even though they were a bit broken up by witnessing a suicide earlier this evening. We've just finished having a bit of a pow-wow about the state of affairs. Tahn will do whatever I do. I'm more than leaning towards leaving regardless of what happens tomorrow. Lauren seems to have already made up her mind. Her Jenolan idea does have some merit, but like Tahn said it could be that plenty of others have already thought to go

169

there, particularly if they've got a hydro plant. I don't know how well the place would go with regards to agriculture, but it is pretty isolated and much easier to defend than this place would be. It would be well worth checking out though. I know there's a major walking track near here that goes right to the place and it couldn't be more than a day or two away. Right now I'm of a mind to find out pretty soon.

Thursday, September 20

Something really bad happened this afternoon. I think more things like it will happen too. It was right in front of us while me and Lauren were talking.

Me and Lauren have been hanging out a lot. Out of all the others I met at the church, she's the only one who seems to do anything. All of them have jobs but I never see them working. She has hardly spoken to Drew for about three days now. I heard them having a fight the other night and later he tried to come onto me while Talon was away. I just played dumb for a while and let him get real close and stuff and then Talon came back and he nearly ran away. Drew's such an arsehole. But worse, everyone's so lazy. Toula was complaining because she had to go down to the creek to get some water and two of the guys were supposed to help fix a fence but they just went off somewhere and drank.

A couple of the really sick people died today. Me and Lauren are starting to get worried that we'll get sick too if we keep working in the hospital. After our shift we walked all the way down to the Three Sisters. Not just to the lookout but all the way to the first Sister. We just sat there and zoned out. We didn't even talk that much, just sat and looked out over the cliff.

Then just before sunset we saw a woman coming down the stairs towards us. It was the woman who freaked out the other day at breakfast. At first we didn't think she saw us. Lauren said her name was Sophie and that she was mental. She came right up to us and asked how we were and we said "OK." Lauren asked her if she was all right and she said "Yeah" and asked if she could sit with us for a while. She just sat there with a sad smile for a few minutes. We didn't even take any notice of her. Then she stood up and said, "I'm going now" and started walking back over the bridge. Lauren leaned over to me and started whispering something and then we looked and Sophie just climbed up on the rail and jumped off. She didn't even scream or anything, just went over the edge. After standing there in shock for a minute, we both went over to see if we could see where she landed, but there wasn't enough light. It was horrible, watching that. When she first jumped, she seemed to hang in the air for ages and then fell like a stone.

We both ran up the stairs and the track back to the road. It's pretty far and we had to stop once we got there. A truck with some of the guys in it was coming down the road and Lauren waved at them until they saw us and stopped. She told them what happened.

"Sophie Mazarakis jumped off a cliff," she said. She told them where it happened.

I sat down on the ground too puffed out and shocked to say anything.

One of the guys started talking into a radio while the others went off with torches back the way we had come.

When they got back, we got in the truck with them and came back here. They couldn't find her either and one of them said that it didn't matter because she was beyond help anyway, even when she had still been alive.

Lauren told me that about three days after the Plague happened, they had found Sophie in a house trying to breast feed a dead baby. She had her husband and son sitting at the table and she was serving dinner even though they were dead. I started crying when I heard that. No wonder she went mental and killed herself. I know I would have too if I hadn't met someone to look after me after Kelly died.

Sophie's suicide has shaken me up pretty bad. Worse than I would have thought 'cause I didn't even know who she was. When Talon came in before to tell us about the meeting tomorrow I was still shaking. That plus the sick ones who also died today has made me think that I don't want to stay here anymore. I know Lauren's going to leave soon and I think Talon is too, but even if he doesn't I might go with Lauren. And I told them that I don't want to work around the sick anymore too. Dr. Cross was sad but she said she understood. I'm sad about it as well but I don't want to risk getting ill now that no one can really do anything about helping you to get better anymore.

I helped the girls pack and made sure they'd got away clean about an hour before sunrise. Neither of them were overly keen to go without me, but I knew that if we all disappeared – me especially – someone somewhere would suspect something. Besides, I wanted to find out how things would go down. I wasn't too hopeful, but if the meeting turned out in a positive way, maybe we wouldn't have to leave at all and I could just go and bring them back. It's fortunate that I wasn't holding out much hope though, because there wasn't really a meeting. It was a shitfight, and I really expected no less.

Clive was checking guns at the door but even if I hadn't been smelling trouble I wouldn't even walk into a pre-school for blind kids without a weapon, so while I made a show of handing over a small automatic, I was careful not to let him see me smuggling one of the Magnums into the building. Clive's not exactly the sharpest tool in the shed, so it wasn't that hard. About half of the town was already there when I arrived, although I couldn't see either Robert or Heather, or Mitchell, which made the alarm bells I'd been hearing ring quite a bit louder. Scott was there, and he was looking as uneasy as I felt. I was glad the girls were gone. After I'd been there a few minutes, he called me over and asked me where Tahnee was.

"I sent her away," I said honestly. "Her and Lauren took off earlier. I'm not going to tell you where."

He nodded.

"Why didn't you go too?" he asked.

"I want to see how things turn out," I replied.

"It's not looking good so far. You got a gun?"

"Need you ask?" I said, and moved away a few feet so I could see the door into the room. Pete and one of the other guys had rounded up the shitkicker kids from the church and were leading them into the place. Lauren's dickwad boyfriend was looking around trying to find her. I waved at him and he flipped the bird.

"Where is she?" he said, accusingly, as he stalked over to me.

"Fucked if I know," I said. "Staying the fuck away from you, obviously. Smart move I reckon."

"Get fucked," he said.

"I already have," I replied in a low voice. "Gave her every inch of it."

Simply for my own amusement, I added, "That Lauren's a good root, isn't she?"

He looked at me for a moment like he wanted to take me on, but didn't quite know how. Then he decided that the best way was to explode into a flurry of blows. He was wrong. I grabbed one of his arms and jerked it around behind his back, then twisted it until he fell to his knees.

"Go and sit down boy," I told him. "I haven't really fucked her... yet."

I let him go and watched him slink over to a chair nearby. As he looked back at me, I winked. I was pretty sure this 'meeting' wasn't going to end well, so I figured I might as well enjoy myself while I could.

I looked back up toward the door just in time to see Heather coming through it with Mitchell right behind her. Coleman wasn't with them, and I got the impression that by the look on her face it was quite possible that not only was Coleman not with them, he was no longer with us. I was wrong about that as it turned out, but right at that moment I thought I'd seen the last of him. It was clear that Scott thought the same.

Behind them was a mob of Mitchell's cronies. There was about twenty of them, and I found myself wondering just how a guy with a master's degree in being a cocksucker had managed to find himself such a following in a few short hours. Poor old Clive was trudging forlornly among them. As he entered the room he flopped down on a chair looking like the most miserable person in history. The rest of the group spread around the room while Mitchell himself led Heather to the front of the gathering. A murmur had started and was beginning to reach a crescendo. People began looking around at each other, at the door, at Scott. A couple of them looked at me. I just shrugged.

The school teacher tried to settle the crowd.

"Quiet please, everyone! Quiet please!"

She could hardly be heard over the noise and at first, no one took any notice.

"Please," she tried again, a little louder this time. I had to admire her for trying to keep it together, because she looked like someone who knew they were just about to get their brains blown out. "Please, everyone be quiet!"

Gradually, an uneasy silence began to fall. As the last of the muttering died away, someone demanded to know what was going on.

Heather plucked up some enormous courage. As if she was addressing a school assembly and about to introduce a cricket hero, she said, "Please pay attention while Mr Mitchell explains what's happening."

She took a small step to one side and I realised that her right wrist was attached to his left with some kind of wire or cord. He'd fashioned a cuff to his end so it wouldn't chafe or cut his skin but he hadn't shown the decency to do the same for her.

Mitchell started to speak.

"First of all, I think you should all know that Bob Coleman is no longer in charge here. I am. If any of you don't like that idea, the door is behind you. You have two hours to leave town. If you require it, we'll even provide a few days' supplies to help you on your way. Feel free to leave now if that's your plan."

He paused and the meeting looked around at each other. A man at the back asked, "Where would we go?"

"Wherever you like," Mitchell continued. "There's bound to be other towns taking in survivors. Of course, you don't have to go anywhere, but I thought it was fair that I give you all the option of leaving now, because I've decided there's going to be some changes as to how things are run around here and if you're not into it, you can go find some other place to live."

"Can't we at least wait until we find out what the changes are?" the same guy wanted to know. He was obviously an idiot.

"Of course. That would make sense, but all I'm saying is that if anyone's got a problem with me taking over from Bob, you might as well go now."

He paused again and waited. No one left of course, which was just as he thought. Then he looked and Scott and I.

"What about you two?" he said.

"I'm quite comfortable where I am, thanks," I said. I folded my arms and slouched back against the wall. "Carry on."

I don't know why, but I wanted to see where this would go. Mitchell was reminding me of our friend the cult leader back in Sydney, but considerably more deranged. He was right that things needed to change, but I was pretty sure that turning up to a town meeting with a gang of gun-toting hoods and a woman handcuffed to his wrist wasn't the sanest way of making his point. In any case, now that I think of it, I doubt very much if he would have let me walk out that door unmolested.

He went on.

"Yesterday some of us suggested that a few changes needed to be made about how we were going to get ourselves out of this mess. Scott and Willis over there" – he gestured at us with a nod of his head – "suggested that we have a meeting today and discuss some new ideas. That's all well and good, but I used to be a bureaucrat in another life so I know how long it can take to implement things that come up at meetings. Extreme conditions demand extreme responses, and in this case, I've decided that what needs to happen is that someone strong takes control and makes the decisions for you. Maybe one day, we can get back to a democratic process, but for now we need a leader who's going to make sure that things get done."

Despite the obvious fear and uncertainty that had settled over the room, there was murmuring again as he said this, murmuring that grew louder and angrier. Scared they most assuredly were, but these were still people who weren't used to be dictated to by a man with a gun, and the shock of seeing Heather being dragged into the place by this guy had worn off. No matter what had happened in the last few weeks, this was still Australia, and Australians were used to choosing their leaders, not having one thrust upon them. They hadn't minded Coleman because he was pretty easy going and as a cop he was an authority figure anyway. Mitchell was just a bully who'd spent most of his life being a nobody in some faceless organisation somewhere.

"I have a question!" I shouted above the noise from the floor. The crowd settled slightly and looked at me.

If he'd thought about what sort of thing I might say, he probably would have ignored me, but the revolt from the crowd he figured he had subdued with this sudden show of force must have rattled him for a moment.

"Yes?" he said. "What is it?"

"How come you're not wearing a Nazi uniform?" I said.

Someone cheered and a few people laughed and shouted. A few men got up and began to rush the front while a bunch of others started to move on Mitchell's drones along one wall. None of them seemed to know how to react, and it looked like Mitchell's little coup was going to be over within seconds. I had just begun to reach behind me to pull the Magnum out of my pants when, all of a sudden, somebody started firing a machine gun into the roof above our heads. People ducked for cover and screamed, then went very quiet. I looked over at the shooter and suddenly recognised a man who was undoubtedly far more insane than

Mitchell himself. I'd noticed him from time to time over the past few days and figured he was pretty shady because he never seemed to make eye contact with anyone, but I hadn't taken much interest in him before. A chill crept through me. This lunatic was Ronald Arthur Parry, one of the worst and sickest killers in Australian history. I'd written a piece on him once for a true crime website.

Sixteen years ago, Parry had kidnapped a middle-aged woman and her twenty-year old daughter from a highway while they waited for road service. He kept them for three weeks, raped and brutalised them, then handcuffed them together, gagged them, zipped them up in a sleeping bag and threw them off a bridge into a river. He was supposed to be serving a never-to-be-released sentence, which meant he should have died from the plague in Goulburn a fortnight ago. How he'd managed to get out of prison I couldn't even imagine, but he was one seriously psycho fucker that even I wouldn't fuck with. I couldn't be sure if Mitchell knew who he was, but it struck me as strange that Coleman hadn't recognised him and put a bullet in him immediately.

"Sit down!" Mitchell roared. Parry had his weapon trained on the crowd and a couple of his buddies had regained their composure enough to do the same.

"Everyone sit down and shut up! This isn't a fucking

circus! Those days are over. There isn't going to be anymore bludging or whinging about who does what and how things get done. The only way any of us are going to stay alive in this town is through hard work and doing what you're told, when you're told. I didn't take this kind of action spontaneously. I did it because it had to be done, and someone had to do it! Coleman was too soft, just prepared to let people do whatever they liked. That's never going to get this place up and running again! People have to work. They have to be tasked and someone has to make damn sure they do their jobs. I'm sorry it had to come to this, but it was never going to work the way things were being done before: people constantly wandering in, straining resources, half the people working their arses off and the other half just moping about feeling sorry for themselves. Now, please, just think about this for a minute…"

He paused for a moment, and released the cord on his wrist so Heather could move away and sit down in a corner. The crowd, knowing they were beaten, at least for the moment, settled. The hoods relaxed too, all except Parry. He walked over and stood in the back corner, peering about with a look of evil on his face.

Someone was going to have to kill that motherfucker.

"We haven't had an earthquake here, or a war. We still have buildings, shelter, food, medicine. There isn't much, but there's enough for us, the people in this room, to keep going for a long time. And we don't have electricity, but we still have plumbing and we still have the means to keep fresh water coming in from the reservoirs. We just need to keep them working. But everyone has to get involved."

His manner was more conciliatory now, but it was clear he was being no less dictatorial. He wasn't about to brook any disagreements with his plan. It's true that what he was saying made sense, but even history's greatest madmen made sense some of the time. Mitchell's ideas – some of which were mine – were fine. His method of carrying them out were deplorable. They were going to get worse too, as we were all soon to discover.

He took out a folder and opened it on the long wooden desk beside him that Coleman used to sit at and drink brandy while he dithered over engineering diagrams and pretended he was rebuilding civilization. Coleman had been about as effective as a leader as a monkey dressed in a sailor suit it was true, but people liked him and he had others around him like Scott and Heather who gave him advice and kept things running, even if it wasn't very well. The town needed a real leader, and Coleman wasn't it. But neither was Mitchell, and I wasn't about to put up my hand either. I wondered for a moment if his offer to leave town still stood.

"Now I've got a list here of everyone, and what your skills and areas of interest are that you gave to Coleman, so I've split people into teams commensurate with their expertise. Pretty soon, I'll start dividing you all up and I'll be assigning some of my team here as supervisors for each of your workgroups."

To me, that sounded like a typically bureaucratic thing to do, and an unsurprising move for the man. It struck me, however, that he'd evidently put a lot of thought into this and had probably been thinking of it for a lot longer that anyone could have suspected, perhaps almost as soon as he got here or maybe even before. While I was thinking this, I noticed some of Mitchell's "team" walking among the assembly handing out small pink envelopes to some of the women. A couple of the girls looked blankly at them, turned them over, opened them, found nothing inside and shrugged. The selection of women who got the envelopes appeared to be random and ad hoc, as if the men giving them out were choosing who to give them to as they went. Which is exactly what they were doing.

"Can I ask all the women who received pink envelopes to stand up please?" Mitchell said.

Slowly, they all got to their feet. A quick headcount showed me there were twenty-two of them. I didn't need to guess how many of Mitchell's men there was.

"Excellent," he said. "You ladies have been chosen to

do work here in the hotel. Heather is going to be your team leader, so I hope you'll all be able to work together with her in any tasks you may be set."

They all looked uneasily at each other. A couple of them weren't much older than Tahnee, none of them could have been older than 25, and all of them were lookers. Only a complete fucking idiot wouldn't have guessed why they had all been picked out and it didn't take much imagination to figure out what sort of tasks they might be set.

"I'd like you all to go with Clark and Aboud now please ladies," said Mitchell.

At first, none of them moved. They all looked around at one another again, then at me, at Mitchell, anywhere except the door. Parry walked up to one of them, a petite, peroxide-blonde with tits that looked too big for her, and backhanded her face.

"That wasn't a request," he said, the first words I'd ever heard him speak.

My gun was in my hand and pointed at the back of Parry's head in less than a heartbeat. I had taken two steps towards him and snapped back the hammer before anyone else did anything.

"If you move again I'll give you the bullet the cops should have given you sixteen years ago, you fucking gutless piece of shit," I said.

It didn't concern me that Parry had a machine gun,

because right now it was down by his side and both his hands were up and away from it. He would have to be Superman to move them fast enough to swing the gun up and shoot me before I could blow his head off from here.

I heard guns coming up from all over the place, pointing in my direction. I felt like Ned Kelly, except I was only wearing a leather vest instead of iron plating and no one was actually shooting at me yet.

"Put the gun down Willis!" Mitchell demanded from the other end of the room.

If I hadn't been concentrating on the back of Parry's head, I would have shot Mitchell instead. No one had called me that since I was in high school and some gormless little ingrate had constantly taunted me by saying "Watchu talkin' 'bout, Willis?" in a Garry Coleman voice until I'd snapped one day and put him in hospital. Now this arsehole had said it twice in half an hour.

"Do you know who this cunt is?" I said. "This is Ronald motherfucking Parry!"

Even Dan Mitchell didn't have to ask who that was. It was like I'd just declared that Osama bin Laden was standing there. I could feel the entire room become instantly stunned.

"Really..?"

Mitchell's voice was a mixture of quiet awe and utter

astonishment.

Sweat had broken out all over Parry's face. I took two more steps and pressed the muzzle of the Magnum up against the back of his skull.

"Scott," I said. "Get his gun off him."

Parry was a maniac, but he wasn't a stupid maniac. He knew that the only person in the room who wouldn't hesitate before pulling the trigger if he did anything foolish was the guy with the gun to his head right now. He let Scott take away his weapon.

"Get on your knees you sack of shit," I said. He sank to the floor and I started yelling at Mitchell without taking my eyes of this scum of the Earth. "Let me fucking kill him! Order me to fucking kill him!"

Suddenly someone shouted "Now!" and from the corner of my eye I saw people surging toward Dan Mitchell. I looked up for the briefest of moments and saw about eight boys, including Lauren's shitkicker boyfriend, rush the guy and start punching the shit out of him. Scott of course now had a machine gun, and while the boys jumped Mitchell, he covered Mitchell's hoods. As it happened, Pete had also smuggled a hand gun into the place, and he was covering them as well. It looked like a scene from Reservoir Dogs. Guns were pointing everywhere. The two losers Mitchell had called Clark and Aboud suddenly dropped theirs and ran out of the room. Clive picked one of them up and

187

before I could do or say anything he walked over to Parry and smashed him in the side of the head with it.

Parry slumped forward onto the ground with his arse in the air. I stepped over the bastard.

"Nice work," I said to Clive.

It was all over pretty quickly after that. Mitchell's goons got tired of pointing their guns at Scott and Pete and eventually they just put them all down. The boys had stopped bashing Dan Mitchell by then, and were standing around high-fiving each other. The girls who'd been selected for "special duties" were huddled together crying. Heather was looking at a spot on the ceiling. Parry was unconscious and Mitchell looked like he'd been run over by a truck. Everyone else was just milling around in shock.

After a couple of minutes, the shock began to subside and anger and indignation began to return. Some of the men picked the guns up off the floor and began to threaten Mitchell's goons with summary execution. The women spat on them and the big-titted chick who'd been slapped by Parry kneed one of them in the balls. I looked at Scott, then at Pete. They were both looking at me. Clive was standing beside me holding his rifle like it was an axe.

I rolled my eyes and fired the Magnum at the ceiling. Someone screamed "Fuck!" and another gun went off somewhere. A guy yelped in pain and tumbled over backwards with a head wound. It was one of the goons, so I didn't care much.

A second later, an uneasy silence descended.

Scott looked at Clive.

"Go get a truck," he said to him, softly. Then, louder: "OK everyone, relax. First of all, I want everyone who isn't me, Pete or Talon and who has a gun, to come over here and put them on the floor."

Hesitantly, the others began to comply, and pretty soon there was quite a pile of hardware at Scott's feet.

"Dr McArthur, do you think you could..?"

He gestured towards Mitchell and the guy who'd been shot. McArthur took one look at the second guy and decided not to bother. He knelt beside Mitchell and began looking him over. While he did that, Scott and I ushered the rest of the villagers out of the hotel and told them all to go home and come back again at the same time tomorrow for a real meeting. They went away in twos and threes. I wouldn't be surprised if some of them moved on now.

Back inside, Pete was covering the goons with Parry's machine gun. McArthur had moved Parry into the coma position and was staunching his wound with a shirt.

"This isn't as bad as it looks," he said, looking up as we came in.

"Too bad," I said.

"Mitchell's in a pretty bad way, though. Broken ribs,

possible fractured skull."

"What a shame," said Scott. He started to say something else, but just then Clive pulled up outside in a large pantec.

"Right." He addressed Mitchell's goons, who were all now sitting around slumped against the wall, feeling sorry for themselves. Pointing to four of them, he said, "You two, take Mitchell. You two, take Parry. Get them and yourselves in that truck out there and get the fuck out of town."

Until he said it, it hadn't occurred to me that might be his plan. I was momentarily dumbstruck.

"What are you?" I cried. "Nuts? You can't seriously be turning these fuckers loose."

I spat on Parry.

"What do you want to do with them? Kill 'em?"

"Only this piece of shit," I said as I lined up the muzzle of my gun with Parry's head.

"It's not gonna happen, Talon," Scott said evenly. "As much as he deserves a bullet, he's not going to get one here. We're trying to get things back to being a little civilized around here, unless you've forgotten. And executing people is barbarism, not civility."

I seriously couldn't believe what I was hearing. I felt like picking up a chair and showing Scott how civilized I could be while I wrapped it around his head.

I tried to tell him once again that keeping a cunt like

Parry alive was madness, but he wouldn't listen. For a few moments I was about to crack a shit and storm out of the place, but I didn't want to look like a childish idiot in front of Mitchell's droogs, so I just gave in.

The droogs got up and started ambling out towards the truck. A pair of them picked up Mitchell and another two grabbed Parry by the arms and began dragging him outside.

I walked out to the bar and dug out a bottle of Scotch that someone had tried to hide behind a loose panel. Pete asked me if I was going to join them outside to make sure the truck left town, but I just smiled at him and started drinking.

A few hours later, Scott, Coleman and Heather came back to the hotel. I think they expected to find me passed out or not there. I gave them a wave and said that I thought it was about time we got serious. The three of them agreed.

Tomorrow, we're going to have a *real* town meeting.

Friday September 21

It was cold and dark when we left to come here this morning. Talon said there might be some trouble at the meeting today so before the sun came up we found this house near the edge of town to hide out in and wait for him to come get us. Lauren cooked some breakfast on a little gas stove and he ate with us and then left to go back to the hotel. I don't really know why he went if he's going to come with us to Jenolan Caves. We could have all just snuck away together while it was still dark. Lauren knows the way to where the track starts so we wouldn't get lost.

While we've been sitting around here waiting, she's been trying to convince me to leave without Talon, but I don't want to do that. I love him. Oops, I said it. Hee hee. I love him and I want to be with him, so even if he comes back later and says he isn't going, then I won't go either.

Lauren's having a nap. She got bored so she went to sleep. I'd like to sleep too, but I can't. I've been thinking about the Plague again. I wonder if, one day, someone will work out what it was. Everyone we talk to seems to think the same thing as me about how people who were drunk didn't catch it, or if they did it didn't affect them. But the real strange thing is that even when we sobered up later, we still didn't catch it and die. That's pretty weird. It's like it was there, infected all the sober people,

192

and then went away again. But where did it go? Dad used to tell me about people with cancer, and how sometimes the cancer can go into remission or become dormant, which means it's still there but it doesn't do anything and then sometimes it comes back worse than before. He also said that sometimes germs mutate into other things and once in a while they might change into something that's not harmful to people.

Maybe that's true but if it is then this bug changed pretty quickly. I can't figure it out. Dara must have already had it when she came to Kelly's that day, and me and Kelly were sober by then, but we didn't catch it off her even though we all slept next to each other. That doesn't make sense, unless maybe once it got inside a person it couldn't spread to someone else somehow. I wonder what Dr Cross thinks. Maybe if we end up staying, I'll ask her.

Later –

Oh well, we're not going just yet. Or maybe not even at all. I'm a bit sad about it because I think I really wanted to go, but I guess it's ok if we stay a bit longer now. Talon wants to give it another chance, so I will too. I'm glad me and Lauren weren't around at the meeting. It sounded like it was pretty scary. I know if they had picked me out to be one of their slaves I would have tried to kill them.

I'm still worried about getting sick from whatever is

putting everyone in the hospital, though. I went and spoke to Dr Cross. She said that she thought it might be something to do with either some of the food people have been eating, something in the water, or maybe a return of the Plague, although she said that if it was that then everyone should be getting it. That's when I reminded her that it didn't seem to affect people who drank alcohol and that everyone here pretty much drinks booze all the time, so that couldn't be it. Then she just looked at me funny and went away. I wonder what that made her think? Maybe she just forgot about that. She is pretty old after all.

It's true about the booze though. Everyone drinks all day, even if it's just a few glasses of whiskey every couple of hours or so. I know me and Talon have a few shots every time we eat and some of the guys just guzzle all day long. Maybe we'll all survive the Plague and die from liver disease.

That just made me think again. If the alcohol is stopping us from getting the Plague, what's going to happen when it all runs out?

Saturday, September 22

The town meeting went over pretty well, considering how things around here have gone over the last few days. Just as I thought, yesterday's events had made people realise that we were all going to have to pull our fingers out if there was going to be any chance of surviving this thing. Quite a few people seemed to have ideas and as dumb as some of them were, we gave them all a chance to speak. Even so, it was Scott and myself, Coleman, the doctors and a couple of other people who did most of the talking.

One of the first things we decided was to take dog and cat off the menu, and no one seemed too upset by that. Culling the ferals is still going ahead, however. It's going to be a struggle for us to find enough meat as it is without having to compete with other predators, especially ones that would eat us if they got the chance. Dogs are pretty handy animals to have around though, so won't be killing them all. Over the last few days some of the people here have rounded up a few of the strays that were still a bit people friendly, and yesterday one of the guys found a litter of puppies in a yard.

The main concern for most was the question of the food supply. Fresh meat isn't that difficult to find; the dams and lakes are fairly well stocked with eels and fish and possums and roos are fairly plentiful. The big problem is with fruits, vegetables and cereals. The nurseries have plenty of seeds and seedling plants, but they'll all take time to cultivate to the level needed for an adequate supply. A couple of people suggested, pretty sensibly when you think of it, that we should look at gathering wild food from the bush. If the Aborigines could live off the land for centuries it makes sense that we can too, as long as we know what to look for. As it turns out, it appears that no one's much of an expert on the subject.

Lucky for us, there's not only a library in the main street but a couple of enormous second-hand book stores that combined together probably hold the entire wisdom of mankind and other things besides. I remember going into one of them once, years ago when I was doing the tourist thing with a chick I was screwing at the time, and just about getting lost in the place. If we can't find all the knowledge we need from the book shops in Katoomba Street, we might as well all follow Sophie Mazarakis' lead and take a swandive off Echo Point.

As easy or as difficult as gathering food from the bush might prove to be though, we're going to need shitloads of it, and it's going to have to be collected every day. When the idea came up, there was a good supply of volunteers for putting the plan into action. Knowing what I know about the people around here though, I can't help wonder how enthusiastic they're going to be after a week or so of traipsing around the bush collecting nuts and picking fruit for hours on end, every day.

Our energy resources are also pretty limited, and it's only going to be a matter of time before we've used up all the gas and other fuels that we've managed to scrounge together. It turns out though that this was one thing that Coleman had actually been devoting some thought to in between maintaining his port intake, and several guys have already been doing some research into building small scale hydroelectricity plants that could utilise some of the nearby waterfalls.

All the sick have been moved from the Carrington to one of the big sandstone churches down the street where they'll be away from the communal areas. Why no one had thought of this earlier has got me beat, but at least it finally has been done.

The chief concern from my point of view however, is defence. There can be little doubt that this isn't the only place in the world where people have begun to resettle, and there's even less doubt that now we've all been reduced to a tribal existence once more, with all of our modern conveniences, luxuries and ways of life relegated at least for the moment to history's filing cabinets, without a national government to hold us all together and with the possibility of starvation and death from inadequate resources hovering over our heads, that the tribes are likely to rub together the wrong way when the time comes for them to start rubbing together. And with every passing day, that time draws closer. Worse, I can't help but keep getting a bad feeling about Mitchell and his droogs. Scott can have all the civility he wants, but letting that bunch off like that could have been the worst call he's ever made in his life.

Right now, I'm just taking a break from poring over maps of the local area. I've got Clive and the little shitkicker who wanted to fight me yesterday, Drew(?), putting together an inventory of explosives and other goodies we can use in the case of attack. There seems to be quite a lot of it.

Only the other day I found out where it came from. Scott, Pete and Clive are all ex-Army or Reservists who spent weekends on a property in Bell with a bunch of mates playing war games with live ammunition and over the years they'd somehow managed to amass the sort of arsenal that would have got them arrested as terrorists if it had ever been discovered. They weren't the sort of right-wing fruitcakes that used to go around worrying about being invaded by Indonesia apparently, more just a group of blokes running around in the bush shooting things and blowing stuff up, like *Quake* or *Doom* or *Halo* something, but with real guns and bombs, which I can fully appreciate. Also, Coleman's police files held some reports about a few survivalist nuts living in isolated places here and there. Ironically, they were all preparing for either some kind of invasion or a natural disaster about ten times worse than the Indian Ocean tsunami a while back and not some kind of alien super-plague, so they all died within hours. The locals just went out to their bunkers and picked them clean.

My first idea was a build some kind of physical barrier around the whole town, but that would take months and we probably don't have that long. Even if we did I'm not sure it would be possible considering the local topography.

So now I'm thinking that we need to cut ourselves off somehow. From what I can tell, it would be a whole lot easier if we were a little further down the mountain where there's not so many roads leading into the place. West of town isn't so much of a problem because there's only one road between here and the next village and from what I remember of it, it wouldn't take much to make it impassable.

Unless someone gets themselves a helicopter, the only way up here in any sort of large group would be via the highway. The countryside is too rugged, wild and steep for an overland sortie by anything less than pretty well-trained commandos, and something tells me there isn't too many of them left these days. When Tahnee and I were walking up this way, I seem to remember that the road coming up out of Faulconbridge went through some rather high cuttings on the ridge. Clive was just telling me too that from the water-tower at Wentworth Falls, there's an almost unrestricted view to the east. I'm going to take a bike out soon and scout a few places. With enough explosives, railway sleepers and any other rubble or junk we can find, we might be able to make the highway impassable enough in a few spots to make a direct assault pretty difficult. We could probably even fortify them to hold off anyone who still wants to make the attempt.

There's still plenty of other people about out there. We pick things up on the radio a lot. Most of the time it isn't much, just madness or ranting like the kind of stuff Steve Davison described. I halfway hope to hear him or one of his mates on from time to time, but if they're still alive down there they're not telling anyone where they are. And a good thing, too.

Back to work.

Wednesday September 26

Ever since the weekend everyone has been working pretty hard. Talon has been working so hard that I've hardly seen him in days, and when I do he's always so tired he barely stays awake long enough to eat. I feel sorry for him, but at least he's getting things done. We've all got jobs to do. Me and Lauren and two other girls have been going through the library and all the bookstores and collecting all the books we can find about survival, defence, building and stuff and moving them all to the community hall and then sorting them out. It's taken a long time. Yesterday they sent a couple of trucks out to get more books from other places and when we went to the hall today there was a gigantic pile in the courtyard. We just finished sorting them about an hour ago. Now me and Lauren are getting dinner ready and waiting for Talon to come in.

No one stays in the church anymore. On Sunday everybody went out and found a place to live in along the main street. Talon and I moved into a big place above a chemist. Lauren's living with us too. It's all one big room that her and I divided up using some screens that we found in a couple of antique shops. When he got back home on Sunday, Talon said he really liked what we did, even though we didn't really do that much.

Tomorrow Lauren and I will be helping to collect food. We found a lot of books about bush food and how to find it. Some of them even had recipes. At the moment there's a bunch of people making up sheets with pictures and stuff on them to give out so when we go out collecting we know what to look for. A lot of the plants just all look the same to me. I hope I don't pick a bunch of leaves that are poisonous or something.

Dr Scott came by the hall earlier when I was there and said that most of the sick are getting better, which is good. No one's been really sick for a few days either so maybe they were right when they said it was eating dogs and cats that were making people ill. I don't know for sure though because me and Talon ate them too and we didn't get sick and so did everyone else.

Anyway, it seems that everyone is getting on better now they all have proper jobs to do. My job's pretty boring though. It started out OK, but now it just makes my brain hurt. I don't know why anyone would want to be a librarian.

Drew isn't bothering Lauren anymore. Yesterday I saw him with a girl called Susie so I guess he's her problem now. Mind you he's been working pretty hard too because he's been helping Talon and Clive and some of the others blocking the roads off.

Lauren's just called me. She's been reading this big cookbook we found and tonight she made kangaroo stew. I guess it must be ready. Talon should be in soon because it's getting dark outside.

Thursday September 27

When I first started keeping this journal I think it was to help keep me sane. Now that I've been given some kind of responsibility for getting this place up on its feet again I feel kind of obliged to keep a history of it. I've never really been one for responsibilities other than that of looking after myself and the loyalty to the guys I rode with. They'd probably think that I've gone soft now that I'm helping out the kind of drones we used to care so little about, but I have to admit that it's actually made me feel good about myself. There's been some good progress made around here in the last few days, and I'm proud to say that a lot of it has been because of me. Last week I was ready to cut and run, and leave them all to their fate just like I'd always done.

I guess it has a lot to do with being needed, and being part of something again. I never felt needed as a kid, what with my parents practically damning my existence all the time. After I linked up with King and Spud and the others, I felt like I was part of something for the first time in my life; I don't know if I ever felt needed at all because I never really thought about it and to be honest I doubt I could see myself being needed by someone like Chubby or Gonk. Perish the fucking thought!

Then Tahnee came along, and if I didn't need her then she damn well needed me. If I'd have fobbed her off

203

back in North Sydney like I was originally going to she would have been feeding the crows weeks ago. And if I'd done that, I very much doubt I'd be sitting here now. Until I bumped into her I didn't even have a clue where I was going to go next.

She's out now, collecting food with about fifty other people. Before she left this morning we fucked for the first time in days. She was a bit worried we might possibly disturb Lauren, and I reckon we probably did, but that was the least of my worries. I think I have a fair to even chance of being able to slip it to Lauren too if I could get her alone somewhere but I really don't fancy the tension that would create.

Funny, it wasn't that long ago I wouldn't have cared about something like that either!

Until today I've hardly had the time to scratch my arse. I've only got the time today because Scott's ordered me off the job until tomorrow. I can't say I'm not glad for the rest, but if he hadn't taken over for the day himself I would've passed on the break and kept at it. I'm pretty happy with the progress so far, although for a while there I was really in a bind about what to do.

After I looked at the maps on Saturday, I decided to go down to just below Woodford and take a look around. The road there goes through a cutting about four storeys high on both sides, and at first I figured we could probably sink some explosives into the cliff faces and

204

bring them down over the highway, blocking it off. Then we could build a rampart on top of the rubble and keep a patrol there. It was only when I got there and actually checked it out that I realised that bringing down a rock face like that properly would need someone who had some skill in explosive demolitions. It was also quite a long way from Katoomba. Even if we just built a wall across and left some guys there, should they be attacked, it would be fifteen minutes or more before anyone could get there to help them. It's a shame, because it's quite a defendable location. We may still be able to make use of it, especially if we get some kind of advanced warning of trouble because, like someone would say if this was some 1950s Western, it's the perfect place for an ambush.

On the way back from there, I found a preferable if not better spot; a point just before it begins the steep climb up Bodington Hill where the highway, the railway line and a smaller secondary road all come close to each other at almost the same level. Putting a wall or something across here would be feasibly easier than trying to figure out how much explosives to use to bring down a few thousands tons of rock. Safer too. It didn't take me long to find building materials either. Quite conveniently, the highway was divided by a wall of concrete barriers about a metre and a half long by a metre or so high. It ran for about a kilometre down the hill, so there were plenty to go around.

Ripping up the railway would provide even more concrete and steel, certainly more than enough to close the way off pretty decently.

Once I got back to town, I decided to get started straight away, so I rounded up the team who'd volunteered: Clive, Drew and a few of his mates. Within an hour, armed with a couple of trucks, wrecking bars, sledgehammers and wheelbarrows, we were at work.

It wasn't easy. The blocks are fucking heavy, and a bitch to move and lift without a crane, which we don't have. But if the ancient Egyptians could build pyramids out of massive blocks of granite centuries before the invention of the wheel, we felt sure as fuck could build a wall from a few blocks of concrete without a crane.

Even so, even with twelve of us prying them loose, loading them up and moving them around, we'd only managed to get enough of them to block the railway by nightfall on Monday. Working out the best way to move them, and then stack them once we got them to the site, took out a big chunk of time. Then we had to deal with the railway itself. That turned out to be a breeze compared to moving the blocks.

By Tuesday afternoon we had about a hundred metres of track torn up and a big pile of sleepers to add to our collection. That was when we suddenly realised that we had a huge Chinese puzzle that no one knew how to put together. I have to admit that I'd gone into this without much of a plan, because I didn't feel there was that much time to come up with one. I was hoping that it would all come together on the fly, and between twelve of us we'd come up with something. But the late afternoon was closing in, and all we could do was sit around and stare dumbly at piles of sleepers, rails and wedge-shaped sections of crash barrier slabs as if we were waiting for them to assemble themselves. For the wall to be any good defensively, it was going to need to be at least two metres high, and that meant finding some way to stack the wedges on top of each other. Except they're completely the wrong shape for that to work. It was looking pretty hopeless. At this rate, we'd have a wall 400 metres long that a kid could jump over. Some defence that was going to be.

For a while we just stood around, watching a team of scavengers go down into Lawson and Hazelbrook, salvaging whatever could be pried loose. From the way the trucks were loaded up on the way back, that was apparently quite a lot.

It was Drew who solved the problem. He'd been trying to get into my good books for a few days now, and to his credit he seems to have really been giving our dilemma some thorough consideration. After the last of the salvage trucks rumbled on past, I watched Drew get up from where he'd been sitting and, without a word, walk over to a pile of sleepers, pick up two of them and lay them laterally across the top of two of the barrier wedges that were standing beside each other looking totally useless.

"Now we can put another row on top," he said, and he was right.

I would have kissed him except I remembered what a fuckwit he could be, and that he was a bloke.

By late yesterday, we finally had more than half the wall built. The boys will probably all but finish it all off today and then we can start on the reinforcement.

It's nice to have a day off though. I haven't done physical work like that in years and my upper body feels like I've been doing weights for about a week solid, which in a way is true. Plus, I haven't had a smoke in almost a week and I already feel like I never had one in my life. If the world ever gets back to normal, I'll be one fit motherfucker.

Friday September 28

Me and Lauren have left Katoomba. We left late this morning with Pete, Dr McArthur and this couple called Tara and Greg. I left a note for Talon saying where we are going, and why. When he reads it, I guess he'll make up his own mind whether to come follow us, or stay where he is. I hope he comes. I can't stay there anymore. It just doesn't feel right.

It was sad to say goodbye to Dr Cross. She has been nice to me. We're not going back to Katoomba and she's too old to travel far, especially now that you have to walk everywhere. Lauren and me are going to Jenolan Caves, just like we planned, so I probably won't see her again.

We have been walking for about three hours now I think. We probably would have gone further but a real bad thunderstorm came up just a little while ago and we had to find some shelter. There isn't any rain, just a lot of lightning and noise. Thunderstorms don't usually freak me out, but this one is pretty bad. Being out in the middle of the bush with lightning coming down everywhere is really, really freaky.

Wow! There was just a big crash pretty near us. I think a tree must have got hit by lightning or something. Tara and Greg have two dogs with them called Jake and Shadow and they are totally losing it, especially Jake. He is so scared, poor thing.

So anyway, it's because we met Tara and Greg that we decided to leave today. Talon had already gone out to work on the defence wall and me and Lauren had some breakfast and were going up to the hotel to see if we could get a new job to do. Sorting and stacking all the books is sending us mental so we going to go ask Heather if there was something else we could do instead or maybe go back to helping Dr Cross. When we got up to the hotel, Shadow and Jake were tied up to a post near the door. Jake jumped up on me and I gave him a pat on the head. It was nice to pat a dog again, instead of eating it. We went inside to see whose dogs they were, and just as we walked in Pete almost knocked us over. He smiled and told us he was going to the library and we should come, so we did.

When we got there, Tara and Greg were talking to Scott and Heather. They had just walked to Katoomba from Jenolan Caves where they are living with a bunch of other survivors. They were looking for a doctor or some medicines because they didn't have any. One man living with them had some kind of infection and a lady was about to give birth in a few days. Scott and Heather were just agreeing that they could have some antibiotics and were about to find out if Dr McArthur was willing to go with them and help out for a while. When he got there, he said he would but he would need some help, so we volunteered straight away. Of course we thought they would wait to leave until tomorrow, but they said they couldn't wait another day because it had already been three days since they left and they had to get back as soon as they could. Me and Lauren ran back to the studio, grabbed most of our stuff and met them all back at the hotel. We've been walking ever since and until the storm started we had been making good time.

There was just some more lightning near us. Pete and Greg reckon that it definitely hit a tree and it might even start a fire. I hope that doesn't mean we'll be stuck out here in the middle of a bushfire.

I might write some more a bit later.

Friday September 28

The kid's gone.

She left me a note on the bed telling me that she and Lauren have packed up and gone to Jenolan with Dr McArthur, Pete and some young couple to help the doc deliver a baby or something. Oh well. Good for her. I hope she makes it, the way this weather is right now. She wrote that she'd like me to follow when I can. Maybe I will, I don't know.

I have to admit that I'm pretty surprised she's gone. After sticking around all this time, it's funny that she's decided to take off now. Maybe she knows something I don't. I may sit back and ponder this a bit later. Right now, the thunderstorms have put paid to any more outdoors work we've got planned for the rest of the day, so a few of us are going up to the pub for a drink. The big-titted blond who kneed one of Mitchell's goons in the balls last week – Karen her name is, so I'm told – has been eyeing me off lately. Today she was wearing an Airbourne t-shirt so tight her nipples were trying to bust out and get some air. Now that Tahnee's not around anymore I might help liberate them.

Fuck! By the sound of that, something really close just got hit by lightning. If I didn't know better, I'd almost think this storm has been sent here to harm us. I've counted about ten lightning flashes in the last few minutes and the thunder is making the windows rattle.

Oh well, if this account ends here, you'll know I got hit by lightning on the way to the pub. How fucked would that be?

Monday, October 1

We made it. After the storms, a fire and a big gale that Pete reckons will make some of the fires in the valley worse, the six of us got to Jenolan Caves. There's a bunch of people here, not as many as at Katoomba. Maybe fifty. An old guy who wears a Ranger uniform is in charge I think. At least, he's the one who told me and Lauren that we could have this room. I'm going to try and have a wash soon. I'm so black from soot and dirt that I reckon I must look like a Somalian.

It was a long walk from Katoomba to here. About as long as it was from Steve and Kathy's place up to Katoomba. We nearly didn't get here at all though, because just what I said I didn't want to happen, happened. The lightning started a big bushfire and we almost got stuck right in the middle of it!

At first, there was just heaps of smoke everywhere. It was so thick that we could hardly see or breathe. Lucky, Tara and Greg and Pete knew the way, so we didn't get lost. Then as we started following the track along this ridge, Pete yelled "Look!" and pointed into the bush. There was a big wall of fire coming straight at us. It was still a bit of a way off, but you could hear it! To me, it sounded like the bear from the zoo, roaring towards us. Just thinking about that makes me freak out.

All we could do was run. Poor Jake and Shadow were so scared that they nearly ran off into the bush in panic.

I was pretty scared too. The smoke was getting thicker and making it even harder to breathe. Then all the embers and soot started coming down around us too. Greg started shouting that we had to find some shelter because if we didn't the fire would kill us for sure. We all started getting covered in ashes, and the dogs started yelping because the embers were burning their fur. We saw a house through the smoke so we ran to it. It was in the middle of a field without any trees close, but I don't think it would have mattered. Any shelter was better than standing out in the flames, and the flames hadn't even reached us yet.

Once we got inside, the six of us just went around making sure all the windows and outside doors were closed, then we huddled together in the middle of the big empty living room and waited.

The fire wasn't really that big. We watched it come towards us, and then it began to turn away to the east a bit so it went right past without coming too near to the house. It moved fast. I guess there hasn't been a real big fire here for a long time so there was plenty of fuel for it. I don't know what would have happened to us if it hadn't changed direction when it did. I think we were pretty lucky.

Anyway, the running wore us all out a bit, so we just sat around in the house and caught our breath and recovered from the scare for a while. It was starting to get dark by then anyway, so us girls decided to go make some dinner.

There wasn't much to cook with, just some kangaroo meat and beans and some berries and nuts and stuff, but the three of us started pretending we were cooking in a big fancy restaurant. Tara found an apron in a drawer and put it on and ran out into the other room saying "Can I take your order?" and the guys started ordering all these meals. It was funny. Then Greg said, "Hey the game's on!" and pretended to turn on the TV and the guys sat around pretending to call the game. Pete used to be a footy player, so he kept making tactical comments like "They've got numbers on the right if they kick now!" and then after about ten minutes Lauren came out and said "The Grand Final isn't until tomorrow!" and everyone just went real quiet. I know she meant it as a joke but the Grand Final really was meant to be on yesterday. I wonder if there will ever be another one?

Later in the night after we had all gone to sleep, a really strong gale started blowing. One of the doors on a shed outside blew shut with a loud bang and woke me up, and then Shadow started barking and woke everyone. Pete and I went out and tried to close all the doors to the sheds and other buildings around the farm so we wouldn't be kept awake all night with bangings, but a couple of them just kept blowing open. While we were out there we could see a big orange glow in the east and another a bit to the south. It was moving away from us and back the way we had come.

I so hope that Talon's ok. I didn't want to abandon him but I couldn't stay there and I couldn't wait for him to come back before I left. He's been as good to me as anyone has ever. I just wish my dad could have met him. Dad might not have liked him, but I wish they had met at least.

The next day (that would be today) after we woke up, me and Tara made some breakfast for everyone and she told me about how her and Greg had both survived. They had been camping down at some river near Goulburn and on the night of the comet it had been cloudy where they were. She said Greg was spewing because he had taken a telescope to look at the comet but ended up not being able to see anything. So they started drinking and played Scrabble instead. That's so funny. I wonder what words they made after they started getting drunk.

They didn't leave their camp until the Tuesday morning, and so by that time the plague had already killed everyone. But they didn't realise for a while because they were in the middle of nowhere. It was only when they started to get closer to Oberon that they knew something was wrong. They saw cars and trucks overturned and burnt out and saw smoke coming up from the town and a few dead people. When they turned on the radio and couldn't get anything Greg decided to take a detour around the town along the Jenolan road

217

and when they got there that's when they found out what had happened. They've been living at the caves ever since. At first there was hardly anyone else there except a few of the Rangers who had been having a farewell party for the old guy I told you about and a few hotel guests and staff. Then after a few days some people began drifting in. Tara said that Greg and some of the others used to drive back into Oberon every couple of days to scavenge. They got shot at a few times, but not hit. Then after a while no one shot at them anymore and one day they found the hospital had caught fire. After that didn't go back into town anymore. They just blocked up both roads into the caves with cars and trucks and farm machinery and stuff. She said they could hear other people over the radio in the Ranger station and knew we were at Katoomba but they didn't want to make contact until they really had to. That's when a couple of people got sick and Tara and Greg decided to come to Katoomba and see if we would help them.

"Greg and I were very lucky," Tara said, and she smiled at me and then out at Greg, who was in the other room playing with Shadow.

I guess all of us who are left are pretty lucky, but they are even luckier because they still have each other and their dogs too.

This room is okay. I think it might be a backpacker's room because it only has bunk beds and no toilet or shower. But it's neat and it beats sleeping on the floor or on the ground. Plus it has lights! The lights still work here because of the hydro-electricity plant. How cool is that? I knew we should have come here in the first place.

Right now I am about to go down to the guest house and get some food. I know I should maybe have a wash first but I'm pretty hungry. Then I'll find out what I can do to help out around here. Maybe Dr McArthur would like me to help him but I guess I don't care as long as it's not collecting old books again.

[Passage undated. Possibly October 3 or 4]

Katoomba is history, and I dare say most of everything east of it is nothing but cinders now too. We managed to get some people here to the Caves. As for what's become of the others, I can't begin to guess.

It's been a few days since I've had a chance to write anything, and it's only the glimmer of old habit that's making me do it at all considering how pointless it seems. I suppose that maybe one day, when the next dominant species on this planet comes past the spot, they might find these pages mouldering under a rock or something, miraculously preserved like a 2000 year old bowl of noodles I read about once that someone dug up in China somewhere. Perhaps they'll decipher it all and wonder at the end of it just how humanity managed to stay alive as long as we did. I certainly don't have any idea.

The storm on the 29th was both the cause and the percursor of worse to come. It should have barely surprised me, really. Things have a habit of only ever going from bad to worse to unspeakably bad, and these days when the cards start to fall, they collapse like a row of shithouses.

While the storm played out, I went for a drink in the Old Bank with Drew, Clive and some of the other guys from the wall building crew. This huge guy called Taylor who is a deadringer for Hagrid from *Harry*

Potter and a weedy Pakistani guy with a pencil moustache and a wonky eye named Farooq were shooting some pool. Taylor had wandered into town in the last few days like Big Bad John and just got stuck straight in working his arse off. I liked him. For some reason he'd struck up a friendship with Farooq and the two were practically inseparable.

Karen was watching them play and Farooq kept trying to slyly eye her off, but it was always hard to tell what the googly-eyed bastard was looking at so maybe he wasn't. It did become pretty obvious that Karen was more interested in me than either of them though. I called her over to slam a couple of shots from the thirty or so that Clive and Drew had poured and lined up on the bar. After we'd done about five each, we scurried back to my flat and fucked a couple of times while the thunder outside cracked the sky so loud it sounded like a war had started.

I woke up a few hours later to the sound of Scott's voice yelling at me from the two-way across the room. He sounded pissed off.

I got up to answer him and briefly wondered why Karen hadn't heard it too until I noticed her dancing around the kitchenette in her panties, listening to something on an iPod.

"Talon here," I said.

"Where the fuck have you been?" Scott demanded.

"I've been trying to reach you for twenty minutes. Get your arse up here."

I couldn't think why he wanted me at what was most likely the middle of the night. I ruminated for a second about telling Karen I was going but decided I didn't care less.

When I got downstairs, the bushfire smell was so strong I no longer had any doubt as to Scott's summons. I don't know why I hadn't noticed it earlier.

Out on the street, a ute roared up the street revving its tits off, spotlights ablaze. A few other guys were jogging up the hill towards the hotel and I joined them. As we arrived at the Carrington, three fire trucks hauled into the driveway behind us. Two more were already sitting outside. Taylor was standing next to one. When he saw me, he grinned.

"You're late," he said.

I winked at him and went inside to the library where Scott had his control room set up. He was sitting at the radio with Coleman and a couple of other guys I didn't know wearing volunteer firefighter kits. I no longer needed to ask what was going on. What I did need to know was what we were going to do.

"Oh good, Talon's here," Scott said, rising. He introduced me to one of the fireys called Carlos, a fat old guy I'd always seen lazing about the town doing as little as possible. It surprised me that he'd figured out how his legs work.

Carlos started talking. Some guys had driven out to the fire tower on Narrow Neck earlier; now they were reporting fires all over the place. A couple of small ones along the ridgetop had burned themselves out pretty quickly but in the Megalong Valley a few had met up and were moving slowly westward. There was also a fairly large blaze taking shape south of Mt Solitary. Depending on the winds, any of them could threaten the town at some point.

I've lived in the city all my life until now, so I've never really been too worried by bushfires. Even a couple of the big ones a few years back that made it into the suburbs didn't concern me too much. But now I was holed up in a town on top of a mountain in the middle of the bush. A town full of reprobates and losers who would probably have trouble pissing out a campfire. What hope did we have battling a real blaze?

Carlos agreed with my thoughts. There wasn't much chance of us putting much of a dent on a large bushfire, he reasoned, so the best thing for us to do would be to gather everyone and everything we could to a central location and just protect that from the flames. The Carrington stood alone at the highest point in town. If we ringed it with fire appliances, there was a good chance, he thought, of holding off the main fire front. Knowing as much about bushfires and fighting them as

223

I know about flying to the moon, I decided he was probably right. But I was still interested in other options.

"What if we have to get the fuck out of here?" I asked. "Has there been any thought about where we should go?"

"We did talk about trying to get further west," said Scott, "but unfortunately that's where the fires are…"

"And going back east is hardly an option," I finished for him, to which he nodded. "Even so, as much as Carlos reckons we might be able to make this place safe, I almost got fried a while back when I accidentally set fire to the whole of George Street, so I'm not that keen on getting caught in the middle of a something like that again."

For a moment everyone looked at me like I'd said something outrageous, then bells started ringing in the church down the road and, almost immediately, a huge gust of wind suddenly battered the town like a giant hand. The bells were the signal for people to gather at the hotel. The wind was a signal that things were about to go nuts.

"We could be in trouble," Carlos said, surprisingly drily.

"What do you want me to do?" I asked.

"How would you feel about playing fireman?" replied Coleman.

224

"Give me ten minutes," I said, and started to leave the room.

"We might not have that long."

"Then give me five," I said, and ran back to my flat.

As I raced up the stairs, I startled Karen, who was lying on the mattress with her headphones in. She sat up sharply, for some reason holding a sheet over herself so she looked like some wench in a Vallejo painting.

"What's the matter?" she asked. "It's just the wind. We get gales like this all the time up here."

I looked at her as if she'd just accused me of having no penis. The air was now thick with smoke that smelled heavily of the surrounding bushland, and bells were ringing constantly. I couldn't believe she didn't know what was happening.

I grabbed a big rucksack and tossed in all the clothes within reach, buckled my guns around my waist and grabbed the little box with all the mementoes of the boys in it and turned to leave.

Karen was still sitting there, blinking like an owl.

"Did I fuck the rest of your brains out?" I said.

"What's going on?" she asked, and I wondered if she'd ever had a brain to begin with. All the pussy in town and I had to hook up with the dumbest bitch left on the planet.

"Get your fucking clothes on woman," I snarled. "There's a fire coming."

I didn't wait to see if she understood.

When I got back to the Carrington, there were people everywhere. The wind howled across the mountain and tore at the town. To the west, beyond the escarpment, an orange glow was starting to rise. There was another, brighter glare in the south.

My arms itched.

Scott appeared in the doorway of the hotel.

"Can you go with Taylor and Farooq and help round up strays? The fire front's moving pretty fast and we need to get everyone up here," he said.

I shouted back that I would and ran around to a ute in the carpark with Taylor. As he and I jumped into the ute, Farooq floored it and swung it out of the carpark and onto the street. As we tore down the hill, I saw Karen shuffling up towards the hotel wearing only panties and her Airbourne shirt. A couple of guys ran past her.

We did a quick sweep of the southern end of town where we knew some people were now living. Farooq leaned on the horn and three or four of them stumbled out into the night. With the smoke so heavy in the air, they didn't need much encouragement to jump onto the back of the ute and let us take them to the Carrington. After two more sweeps we were satisfied there was no one left; if there was, it was too late for them.

Inside the main dining room, anyone who hadn't been

volunteered for firefighting was crouched on the floor wrapped in wet blankets and towels. Everyone else had wriggled themselves into ill-fitting firefighting kits and were assembled in the foyer. I was amongst them.

I'd never fought a fire in my life, but now I was left with no choice.

The building had been surrounded as best could be by fire trucks, and each truck had four or five crew. Along with Drew and Clive, I was with one of the crews at the back of the building with an old Vietnamese guy called Than and this curvy Maltese chick called Paula.

Carlos barked out a few final instructions. The crews on the north, east and south sides would keep their hoses on the building, wetting down the walls and roof. The eight crews at the back of the place were to concentrate on the fire front. It didn't matter if we didn't put the fire out. We just had to stop it reaching the hotel.

I picked up my belongings and my weapons and went down to the truck I'd been assigned to crew. I stashed my stuff in the back of the cab and went back up to the carpark to wait with the others. After a few minutes, I went upstairs to the top floor of the hotel where Scott and Coleman were watching the fire.

The wind contined to tear at the town, the constant gale buffetted us with blasts of heat from the flames. Then it topped the ridge and bore down directly on the scattered buildings among the trees to the west. Despair shivered through us. Tree-high flames swept down on the outskirts of town and engulfed everything in their path like eight-year olds skarfing down sweets.

We were struck suddenly with a wall of heat and there were dull thuds in the distance as windows blew out and structures exploded into flames even before the fire reached them.

The new flesh on my forearms tingled and itched.

"We can't fucking fight that!" Scott said in a despaired half-whisper.

It was time to do what I should have done days ago.

"I'm getting the fuck out of here," I said.

After what seemed like only a minute, the fire front had covered a third of the distance between the ridgetop and the hotel. It extended for a kilometre or more to the south, a hungry, terrifying wall of seething orange. Part of it dropped into a shallow gully and for a moment seemed to slow down.

I bolted outside to the truck I'd been assigned and jumped behind the wheel. The other members of my crew stared at me blankly.

"What are you fucking doing, Talon?" Drew said.

"Getting the fuck away from here," I replied.

They all looked at each other, then at me. A heartbeat later, they were all in the cabin of the truck. I turned the key and floored the pedal.

Parke Road is steep. A kid on a skateboard rolling down

from the top could break the sound barrier without much effort. We were going uphill in a modified Isuzu truck carrying 3000 litres of water. Even though were weren't that far from the top of the hill, getting the thing to accelerate was like trying to coax the dead back to life. Like a monstrous snail, the tanker reached the crest. I was vaguely aware of people shouting, some over the radio and some in the truck with me.

I almost rolled it getting past the roundabout. A few seconds later we were over the railway bridge and I threw the wheel to the left. The truck lurched dangerously and I almost rolled it again. The fire was ahead and to the left of us, moving with a terrifying sucking and roaring sound like an immense helldemon, but cut off from reaching us for the moment by the railway cutting. The wind seemed to have dropped a little quite suddenly, but nothing was going to stop the fire now.

I'm blurry on what happened next. I remember Clive screaming at someone over the radio, telling them to get everyone out as fast as they could to the north side of town and Paula, I think, turned on the cab spray. It must have been that, because water starting pissing down all over the truck and it sure as shit wasn't raining. All I was thinking about was getting me as far away from the inferno as I could. I couldn't have given a shit about anyone or anything else. I'd come close to being burnt to death once before, and I didn't want to try it a second time.

I was fucking terrified.

When they finally convinced me to stop, we were somewhere near Blackheath. Clive wanted to murder me, but as I had several guns and knives and he didn't have any, that wasn't likely to happen.

There was silence from the radio at first, but then after a few minutes there were short conversations from other groups and a few minutes after that some fire trucks and a handful of other vehicles started pulling up nearby. I climbed up on to the roof of my tanker and made a show of playing with one of my handguns, just in case anyone decided I should be punished for having been a coward.

No one did. Shortly, about 35 people had gathered around us. Taylor and Farooq were among them and, miraculously, so was Karen. I have no idea how she had managed to get her arse into a car and get away.

The orange glow was in the southeast now, and far away from us. The wind had died almost completely. It was still, dark and silent.

Before long I realised that the truck I was standing on had been virtually ringed by people. In the glow of headlights they were drawn and pale and covered in soot. And they were lost and looking at me.

Time seemed to have frozen, but in reality from the

moment the fire had topped the ridge to when I'd freaked out to right now had probably been about half an hour or so. Once again, these people had lost everything in next to no time.

When I realised that they were looking to me for guidance and not to tear me limb from limb, I groaned. I would have gulped down some whiskey, but I had none.

"OK then," I said with a sigh, "let's go find a pub."

That seemed a good enough plan for the time being. Paula drove and the rest of the survivors tagged along behind.

A short distance further along the highway, we reached the village of Blackheath. It was as dark and quiet as the bush around it. A few cars with skeletons in them were overturned or speared into trees or one another, and some of the buildings had been gutted by fire. The New Ivanhoe Hotel still stood, doors agape. We stopped and Drew and I went inside. We were the only ones who still had guns, so we swept the place before letting the others come in.

The pub had been ransacked, but someone at some point had made a go of tidying it up a little. Who and where they were was anyone's guess, but it had been done some time ago, and there was no sign of anybody about anymore. Had there been, I was sure the noise of a convoy of fire trucks and half-burned utes and cars would have made them either flee or come out shooting.

Despite his reluctance to speak to me, Clive went down into the cellar and managed to dredge up a couple of kegs and three cases of Scotch. I couldn't see the point in the kegs, but the Scotch seemed like a good idea until I actually had some. It was a generic brand that was so bad I almost couldn't stomach it, but I needed a drink.

Than volunteered to go seek out some food and a couple of others put their hands up to go with him. I gave him one of my guns. Taylor moved to go also, but I asked him to stay and sent Farooq and Drew instead.

Just like that, I was now a leader. A man who'd run like a dog from people who had been relying on me, to leave them to quite possibly die horribly. I wondered if I should care, and realised that I should. Scott had been a good bloke and he'd trusted me to help him.

While Than and the others were gone, those who were left just sat around looking traumatised. Everyone was silent. Clive had taken a bottle of Scotch and gone off somewhere with it. Taylor came over next to me.

"Just in care you're interested mate, it wouldn't have made any difference if you'd stayed or not," he said, perceptively. His voice was like the rumble of a distant tide. "There was no way we could have stopped that fire with what we had. Man, we couldn't have even made a dent in it! A couple of teams opened up with hoses but it was like pissing into a blast furnace. Scott was fuckin' mad to think we could just sit it out in the hotel like that. By the time we realised, it was too late."

I didn't bother telling him that staying at the hotel hadn't been Scott's idea.

"Do you think anyone else made it?" I asked.

"Hard to say. After you bailed, people just started freaking out. Me and Farooq jumped in the ute with that chick you'd been fucking and just fucked off. When I looked around, there was a few others behind us in cars and people just running everywhere. I guess if they ran the right way they could have made it."

He shrugged and took a long pull out of a Scotch bottle.

"Doesn't really matter now, does it? We're all just hanging around waiting for the next disaster to kill us anyway."

He took a seriously heavy slug that would have put Chubby or Spud away and shuffled off quietly into the shadows.

Than and the others came back after what seemed like an hour or so, laden with shopping bags full of tins, bottles of water and packets of processed food. I was impressed they'd managed to find so much.

"We should go back tomorrow and get more for the trip," Than suggested.

"What trip?" I asked.

"Trip to wherever we are going," he said. "Only fool

would stay here for long."

I nodded.

"You're right, mate," I told him. "Tomorrow we're heading down to Jenolan Caves. There's people there. Maybe they can help us. If not, we'll find somewhere else."

"Your girlfriend is there?" Than said.

"That's where she went," I replied. "I don't know where the fuck she might be now."

He just grinned at me strangely and went into a corner to cook some beans on a one-burner camp stove he'd obviously found for himself. Than had been a conscript in the North Vietnamese army and was therefore both a resourceful and potentially very useful guy.

I opened a tin of spaghetti and ate it cold, washed it down with some water because the Scotch was so horrible and drifted off.

Early in the morning, I was woken by Clive shaking me. When I saw him looming over me, I sat up with a start.

"We should go," was all he said, and started to walk away.

I called him back and motioned for him to sit down. He didn't look angry anymore, just sad and broken like the rest. I started to speak to him but he cut me off with a wave.

"It's all right Talon," he said. "If you hadn't got us away from there, we'd all be dead now. I heard what Taylor said to you last night and he was right. I just wish we could have got everyone out."

He paused for such a long time that I thought he'd finished. Then he shuddered with a silent sob so violent that it quite possibly made his bones shake.

"Jason was a good mate," he said finally.

"I know," was all I could reply. It was the first time I'd ever heard anyone mention Scott by his first name.

As I got up to get things organised, I heard Clive start to cry.

Before we left, we split up into teams and ransacked whatever stores we thought might have anything useful still left in them. Rather surprisingly, it seemed that until now Blackheath had been left reasonably intact and we could have taken so much stuff that we would have needed a few more vehicles to carry it all. As it was, we took what we could and headed west, keeping a careful look out. The going was slow and more than a few times we had to use the fire appliances to push or tow ruined cars and trucks from our path.

Mt Victoria seemed as deserted as Blackheath had been but as we motored towards the Imperial Hotel, Paula noticed some movement in a doorway and we slowed to a crawl. A couple of windows on the upper floor came open and machine guns began to poke out of them.

"You just keep right on moving!" yelled a voice, and I waved to let its owner know we understood. I caught a glimpse of the voice's owner and was a little surprised to see that he was a soldier. Until now, I hadn't even considered how the military might have been affected or what, if anything, they'd been doing all this time, but it's highly possible that their ranks would have been decimated as much as, or even more than, the ordinary population. Whatever unit these guys had once been from, though, they were obviously no longer in the national service but in the service of themselves.

I wonder how many other units of Army personnel there are scattered around the place, and if any of them were under any kind of official command. If they were, it's highly likely they would be more interested in locking down small strategic areas than fanning out around the countryside trying to restore order. The very fact that this was the first time I'd so much as encountered any gave me an inkling that the Army, and possibly the Air Force and the Navy as well, was probably just as fucked as everyone else. Even if they weren't, trying to restore order out of this chaos was going to take a military far bigger than anything this country has ever had.

We passed through the town unscathed, but I didn't feel comfortable until we began to snake our way down Victoria Pass. Even then I could barely relax, because if there was ever a place for an ambush, this was it.

We reached the bottom without incident though and after a few more unsettling moments as we passed silent and apparently deserted buildings scattered along the highway, our convoy turned onto the Jenolan Caves road.

We followed it at a snail's pace for about an hour. This far from any town, it was just like a regular drive in the country apart from the appalling number of cow skeletons and the overgrown paddocks we passed. At one point, what looked like an army of kangaroos bounded across the road in front of us. Then, as the road narrowed and began to wind down into the valley, we were halted by a bus lying on its side and a pile of car wrecks topped with razor wire. A white car bonnet had been bolted to a large tree. In remarkably neat lettering, a sign had been painted on it that read: "This area is booby trapped. Unauthorised persons will be shot." Underneath was a smiley face with "Have a nice day" written below it. Less distinct was a short list of radio frequencies that appeared to have been scrawled on later, probably by someone who figured that not everyone who came this way was necessarily going to raid the place.

Clive found a channel that matched the radio gear in our truck and with a shrug keyed in the mike.

"Jenolan base, do you copy, over?" he said, for want of

something else to say.

The answer took a while coming.

"This is Jenolan. What is your intention and location, over?"

"Rape and pillage, over," Clive replied drily. He wasn't the only one who thought that was a pretty stupid question.

"Is that you Clive?" said a new voice almost immediately. It was Pete.

"Roger that, mate," Clive said with a grin. "Get your arse out here and bring us in."

An hour or so later, Pete and a group of other men and women pulled up on the other side of the barricade in a Landcruiser. After several minutes, they rolled back the razor wire and clambered across to meet us.

"You know," I said to Pete as he climbed down onto the road, "we could have done that from this side."

"Probably not without blowing up a few of you," he replied. "That sign isn't lying."

By now, the members of our little convoy had all gathered around my truck. Pete did a quick scan of the crowd before asking the inevitable.

"Where's Jase?" he said.

"Scott didn't make it," I answered. "I'm sorry."

He paled and covered his mouth with his hand. After a moment, he stammered, "What happened?"

"I'll tell you on the way," I said.

We negotiated the barricade slowly, lugging over the supplies we'd taken from Blackheath and helping some of the survivors who were almost at the limit of their endurance. On the other side, the weaker ones squeezed into the Landcruiser and the rest walked for a while until the car came back for us. As we went I noticed Than looking around, scouting out the territory. Now and then he'd smile ruefully and nod and when I asked him once what he was smiling at, he pointed up the slope to a large boulder.

"Booby trap," he said.

After that, I kept watch myself, but apart from a rather obvious stick of what appeared to be some kind of explosive pinned to a tree, I couldn't find any sign of danger.

"We had to disarm the traps along the road so we could come get you," one of the Jenolan people said. "That's why it took so long. Once the 'Cruiser picks up the rest of you, we'll reset them all."

Pete was pretty cut up about Scott. Once I'd explained what happened, he sat in glum silence as we rode down the mountainside towards the Caves.

I felt like the biggest cunt left on earth. Then I thought about what Tahnee would do once she found out about Karen, and I felt even worse. As the forest drew back from the road and the Grand Archway yawned from the foot of the cliff ahead to swallow the road, I wished for a moment it could be a black pit opening to swallow me.

Friday, October 5

I thought I would be happy if Talon turned up. Well, I was when he got here but now I'm angry. He tried to come in before but I told him to go fuck himself. He's such a fucking prick. I thought he loved me and last night we made such sweet love that I cried.

Then this morning when we were in the dining room that scrag Karen came over to him and I found out that he fucked her. I was only gone for a day and he already went and fucked someone else. When I found out I picked up a big plate of food and chucked it at her and hit her right in the face and made her nose bleed. She started to come over to fight me but I pulled my gun on her. I was so angry. She is lucky that Lauren was there to stop me or I would have shot her.

Everyone was there looking at me. Talon looked kind of shocked but also like he was going to laugh at me like he did when I nearly shot him once before. Then I ran out and came up here and locked the door.

Lauren came up but I told her to go away. Then Talon came up but I just screamed at him and threw a chair at the door.

I am so nuts. Why should I care about him? There are so many other hot guys around here, like Pete who's wanted to fuck me for ages or even Drew. Drew is a prick too but I would fuck him just to get back at Talon because they are friends now. Except I don't think Talon would care. If he did he wouldn't have fucked Karen. Plus Drew is with Paula now I think and she's nice.

The worst part is that even though I fucking hate him, I know that it hurts so bad because I love him so much. Last night with him was so wonderful even after I had cried so much about Dr Cross and all the others dying that I could have died too right after and I wouldn't have cared.

I am so nuts right now. I am shaking while I am trying to write and there are tears on the page.

I have no heart anymore. I can't write now.

Later– I was sick before. Me and Lauren were in the Devil's Coach House where we like to go and talk when we get a chance and I started to feel really woozy and ill. I sat for a while to see if I would feel a bit better before I tried to go and see Dr McArthur, but then I started spewing up. I didn't eat much earlier so I was just chucking up bile. It was foul. After a while I felt a bit better and I went to see the doctor. He asked if I felt ok now and I said yes, so he said to come back later if I got worse because Mary was going into labour and he had to be there to help her.

I felt all right by then so I went back to help Lauren working on the little farm that we've made down on the old camping grounds. I felt a bit sick now and then since then but I haven't spewed or even felt like it so maybe something just didn't agree with me.

242

Talon's been here and taken all his stuff. The corner looks real empty now without it all piled there. I'm still really angry at him but I miss him again too. Lauren said I should just forget about him but it's so hard. He was so good to me when we were together. Maybe he thought he would never see me again after I left and that's why he slept with Karen. I think when I see him tomorrow I'll try and talk to him.

I feel a bit sick again. I'm going to try and sleep now and see if I feel better in the morning.

PS – Lauren told me before that I actually shot at Karen earlier. I was so angry I didn't even realise. She said I nearly hit Talon. Maybe I should have blown his balls off.

Friday, October 5

Note to self: Don't piss off Tahnee Goss. I should have realised this after watching her kick the crap out of that kid at Acer but after this morning's episode I'm damn sure she's got a switch inside her head that just flips to "crazy" when she gets cranky. It's all my fault of course. And Karen's. It pisses me off when I think that guys like Scott are dead and that bitch it still running around wasting oxygen.

Last night I bribed a guy with a nice bottle of malt whiskey I found and I took Tahnee up to a room on the top floor of Caves House and we fucked for a couple of hours. When we came down for breakfast, Karen waltzed over to me wearing a nightshirt with nothing under it and tried to fuck me right in front of her.

The penny dropped in Tahn's head like an anvil falling out of the sky and she went fucking psycho. She picked up this huge tureen full of pasta and threw it right at Karen. Luckily, only the serving spoon that was in it made contact, but it smacked her right in the face and busted her nose. Then, Tahnee pulled out a gun and shot at her! I couldn't believe it. The bullet actually went so close to me that I heard it go past. Lauren knocked her hand down and then she ran out of the place screaming like a maniac.

For a long time I was so stunned that, after everything I'd just been through I'd almost had my head blown off

244

by accident, all I could do was sit in my chair and gaze into space. Then I went up to Tahnee's room to try to talk to her. Instead of coming to the door, she just threw something heavy against it and screamed, in one of the most evil voices I've ever heard, "I'm going to kill you, motherfucker!"

I decided she needed some more time to deal with the fact that I'm an arsehole and went looking for something else to do. For a moment I thought about taking Karen off into the bush and dropping her down the bottomless pit that I've heard is around here somewhere, but there's a bit of a shortage of women around as it is and every town needs a bike so she probably still has some use.

I still hadn't yet had the chance to acquaint myself with anyone who may have been in charge here because after I'd arrived I'd been more interested in getting loaded and fucking to take my mind off the guilt I felt. If I'd walked out on King or the others like I'd run from Scott and Coleman, I would have been hunted down and killed like a dog.

But Scott and Coleman weren't King or Chook and this morning, after half a bottle of Turkey and a couple of bouts of good hard fucking the night before, I felt better. It's not as if I could go back now and drag them and Heather Barry out into the street and into a truck so they could get away. They had eyes and legs. They

245

should have got the fuck out when they still had the chance.

I figured I might as well go and see whoever was calling the shots around here, so I grabbed a quick shower and headed down the hill towards the guesthouse. The guy I took to be in charge looked a bit like an older, more efficient version of Coleman, so I wanted to put old Topper's hat on, just for giggles, but it was in the room with all my other stuff and a scorned teenage girl with a handgun. I wondered if I'd ever see it again.

As I got near the door to the guesthouse, a slim, small-breasted brunette in brown cargos and a very small black t-shirt came outside accompanied by a floppy-eared kelpie. The dog saw me and trotted over with a goofy look on its face. I reached down and scratched it behind the ear.

The woman said hello and I returned the greeting, making no effort to hide the fact I was checking her out. She didn't seem to care.

"You must be Talon," she said, and I nodded. "Tahnee told us plenty about you."

"Yeah, well right now she just wants to put a bullet in me," I said with a smile.

The dog licked my hand.

"I'm not surprised," the woman replied, and that made me smile more.

"Where can I find whoever's in charge around here?" I asked after a moment.

She pointed across the road to a door in a building with a sign declaring it to be the ticket office on the front. I thanked her and walked past in the direction she'd indicated. After a few steps I looked back over my shoulder in time to see a scruffy-looking guy in an ancient Iron Maiden t-shirt come over to her and give her a kiss. The kelpie ran up the hill a little to where another dog was lying in the sun. They began wrestling.

I walked to the door and went through without knocking. The efficient-looking fellow was sitting behind a desk and glanced up with a start.

"Yes?" he said, with the trace of a British accent that had all but worn off. He gave me a disapproving look over the rims of narrow glasses. He was lean despite his age, which was probably the wrong side of 65, his hair had once been black but was now mostly grey and he was good friends with a razor. His Caves Trust uniform was neatly pressed and ridiculously clean, and he was even still wearing a nameplate that identified him as Leonard Cullen. I wondered if he'd ever so much as taken a piss without ringing head office to ask permission, and now that head office most likely no longer existed, how his bladder was holding up.

A few weeks ago, I would have spat on Leonard Cullen just to see what colour handkerchief he'd use to wipe it off. Now, I just told him who I was and asked if he could give me the low down and maybe something to do.

It appeared my reputation had preceded me, but as I'd only just been involved in a near-fatal shooting in a room full of people, that didn't surprise me very much. Not only that, but a few of the stragglers who'd come in with me had evidently already spoken to him.

"I suspect you're rather good with motorcycles?" he said.

"I do all right," I admitted. "My real forte is killing people."

Even though that was more or less true, I'd said it to amuse myself. Cullen accepted the comment as if I'd just told him his dinner was ready.

"Well with luck you won't have to do too much of that," he replied.

I was impressed. If anyone left on the planet was an exact opposite of myself, it was this guy, but even with a gun-toting teenage girl out for my blood, I felt far more at ease in this place with Cullen running things than I'd felt since the world had gone arse-up.

Cullen estimated that there was currently enough resources for about 150 people to live quite comfortably for the next three or four months, by which time he expected there to have been enough progress with crops, gathering and hunting to keep it going through the winter, which he admitted would be hard. With our group arriving yesterday, local numbers had increased from 56 to 89, so the population was still manageable, plus it meant an increased labour force. The only major concern he had for the present was the lack of medicines and medical staff. Until Dr McArthur had come here with Tahnee and the others, the only people with any medical experience were an assistant in nursing and a retired pharmacist who could hardly see.

We talked for about fifteen minutes, and when I left I felt pretty satisfied that Cullen seemed to know what he was doing and had appeared to put plans into action far better than Robert Coleman could have ever done, although I didn't really buy his line about crops unless they were growing some super-advanced form of plants that sprang from the ground fully laden with fruit within weeks, which I doubted. I also got the distinct impression that he didn't like me much. I'd figured that out right away, of course, but at least he didn't order me to leave so I'm willing to believe that he thinks there might be a use for me here yet. I was a little irked that he didn't assign me anything to do, but that could be because he doesn't think I'm very trustworthy.

Which is true.

I hunted down the bar. Taylor and Farooq were in there, so I had a drink with them and after about an hour went back up to try and see Tahnee again, or at least be able to get my gear back. She wasn't around, so I grabbed my stuff, found an empty room a few doors down and set up shop. The room's ok, but I'd trade it for the studio in Katoomba any day. It reminds me of prison.

Later – I hadn't intended to doze off, but I did. When I woke up, I figured I should scope out the area. If I was right about Cullen, it was vaguely possible to make a go of it here, so I needed to get familiar with the place.

When I stepped into the hall I thought for a brief moment that Tahnee would take another potshot at me from her room, but the door was open and she still wasn't there. I shrugged and went outside.

The sun was bright and high in the sky but it was warm without being hot. As I wandered around I noticed that unlike the Katoomba survivors, hardly anyone was carrying a weapon and almost everyone looked like they actually had something to do. I saw guys pushing barrows loaded with firewood and in an area above the guest and bunkhouses that had once been a carpark, chicken runs and smokehouses for meat had been built and some repairs were being carried out.

It was much the same wherever I looked. People were hard at work doing things, and I felt like a bit of an idler just wandering around aimlessly. I began to wonder where Tahnee was, what sort of job she'd been given, and whether she still wanted to blow my head off or if she'd prefer just to blow me. I'd started out merely with the intention of familiarising myself with the lie of the land, where things were and what went where but after a while I realised that it was Tahnee that I was actually looking for. My guess was she had gone off with Lauren somewhere to bitch about me and plot some kind of ironic revenge and I was half-hoping that I'd bust them getting it on or something.

To be honest, I hadn't really thought much about her after she'd left Katoomba, but seeing her again yesterday seems to have woken something in me. I'm not sure that it's love, because I don't know if I'm capable of that, but there is definitely some kind of feeling there. I certainly felt far worse about her finding out about Karen than I thought I would. I knew I'd feel a little bad because she's a good kid and she'd be hurt, but I actually feel pretty guilty.

I'm sure I'll get over it though, and it's not as if she's the only pussy available.

After grabbing a bite at the guesthouse, I walked through the Grand Arch and had started down towards the lake with a vague idea about checking out this hydro plant that I'd heard about when I came across Drew and Paula having a quiet snog. I hadn't realised they were together but it didn't surprise me that he would have grabbed the first available half-decent piece of tail he could find. She was the third or fourth chick he'd been with since I'd known him.

I asked them if they'd seen Tahnee or Lauren, but they weren't any help. Drew was so busy trying to get Paula's tits unwrapped that I doubt he would have seen the others anyway unless they'd walked past completely naked.

I went a little further down the path towards the dam, then decided I couldn't be fucked anymore and went back to Caves House for a drink. Karen was there and I thought about trying it on her but she took one look at me and fucked off. I stole a half pint of rum while the barmaid wasn't looking and crept back here to drink it.

I've spent the whole day feeling like a fifth wheel and I'm stone fucking bored. Even writing all this isn't keeping me occupied. I felt like going looking for Iron Maiden fan before and asking if he would share his small-titted woman with me but then the rum kicked in and I realised that she isn't what I wanted.

I heard Tahnee and Lauren come by a minute or so ago. I tried to get up and go to the door, but I can't. I'm surprised I can still hold a pen. In fact, I'm surprised I'm still conscious. Won't be for much longer, though.

Saturday, October 6

Mary's baby was born this morning! She had a girl!
When I found out I ran down to Caves House to go see.
Everyone was really excited, but also real worried in
case the Plague was still around and the baby caught it
and died. But she didn't and she's fine and so wonderful
and cute. They named her Eve. Mary let me hold her for
a while and I just sat there staring at her beautiful little
face. She grabbed my finger real tight and I nearly cried.
One of the guys took photos of me with her so once he
prints them out I'm going to stick one in here.
After I gave Eve back to Mary, Dr McArthur asked me if I
had felt sick again and I said that I felt a bit crook last
night but I was fine now. I feel ok now, too, so I think it
might have been something that I had to eat yesterday.
Right now I have to go out with Lauren down to the farm
again and later on I might go see if Talon wants to talk to
me.

Later – It's really late now and Lauren is asleep. I'm not
going to write much now because I've walked pretty far
but he loves me! He loves me, I know it. And I love him
too. Today after I got back from working at the farm,
there was a knock on the door and when I opened it
Talon was standing there with a flower. It looked so silly
that I laughed. He laughed too and then he grabbed my
hand and dragged me outside. He took me up to the top

253

of the hill above the caves and we had a picnic up there with some wine and a little food that we scrounged from the dining room and he said he was sorry that he cheated on me. I said I was sorry that I tried to kill him and he just laughed and said that everyone is always trying to do that so I shouldn't worry. Then we made love again and it made me so happy. I just know that we will be together now and I am happy even though I was sick again today. But it's ok because I think I know why I'm sick and now that I'm back with Talon I don't care.

I think I'm pregnant.

Saturday, October 6

Make-up sex really is sweet. I can't say I ever knew what it was like before because I've never been with a woman long enough to make up with her about anything. I'm still trying to work out how this one managed to get her hooks in me so far. Maybe in the midst of all this uncertainty, I just need someone who needs me. Needing me is a risky business though, so this kid must need me fucking bad.

Whatever, since yesterday I've haven't quite been able to shake from my mind the look on her face when she found out I'd fucked someone else. The stare she had given me when our Satanist friends had been dragging her along the hall at Acer had been like a smile in comparison. So after zonking myself out on Bundy last night and waking up with that look still peering at me through a headache that felt like my skull was being slowly run over by a tank, I felt that the least I could do was something that might make her feel better somehow.

It took me a while to organise it because after I'd clawed myself out of my hangover, a guy called Greg whom I recognised as the one I'd seen wearing the Maiden shirt yesterday, tracked me down and told me that Cullen wanted to see me. At first I thought he might just want me to get a haircut or start wearing a shirt or something, but it turned out that some bikes needed a bit of fixing. I knew there were a couple of mechanics around because at least one had arrived here with me and I wondered why he hadn't asked them to do it but at least it meant I wasn't going to be sitting around bored fucking stupid all day.

I'm not a mechanic but if there's one thing I do know a bit about it's bikes, and even though these weren't the sort I'm more familiar with I gave them a bit of an overhaul and tinkered around with them for a while.

About midday I went down to the guesthouse to see if I could dredge up a decent bottle of plonk. The only thing I know about wine apart from how to get it out of a bottle is that some of it tastes all right and some of it tastes like a cat pissed in it, but either kind will get you pretty stonkered if you let it. I decided the best thing to do was to ask at the bar what one of the good-tasting ones was, but the tricky part would be actually getting it out of them.

Unlike at Katoomba, Cullen has a rather strict rationing policy going, especially when it comes to alcohol, which is why I'd had to steal the rum yesterday. By all accounts, measures have been put in place to create our own supply of booze, but the way most people I've met lately drink, the stuff already available is certain to run out a long time before the home-made variety can replace it. Even if they'd started brewing and distilling the day after the plague hit, a month is hardly long enough to brew a few bottles of decent beer let alone enough booze to keep a hundred people in their cups.

With a bit of sweet-talking I was able to wrangle a Coonawarra red and two glasses out of the chick in the bar. She had to actually go out into the cellar to get it. No one else was around, so while she was gone I filled King's flask with Jack. At least if the wine tasted like shit, I would still have something to drink.

I didn't think I'd have much luck commandeering anything out of the dining room staff. The woman who runs it is like Nurse Ratched and makes damn sure Cullen's ration rules are carried out to the letter: three meals a day, no more and nothing in between, unless it was on doctor's orders. Only the guys on sentry duty got to eat pretty much when and as much as they liked. I thought briefly about going in there and telling them that I'd been appointed to the sentry team, but Cullen and The Matron are thick as thieves so she'd most likely have known that was a lie. As it was, I just grabbed some lunch then stashed the wine in my room and went back to working on the bikes.

I didn't get much done. Maintenance and modification had been Toolbox and Grogan's area in the old days and the boys had always given me strife about being one of the least mechnical out of us all. I stuffed around for a while until I saw Gresik or whatever his name is from the Katoomba refugees and left them for him to do. Then I went to see Cullen again to put up my hand for sentry duty.

"How did you get on with those motorbikes?" was the first thing he asked.

"I think they might be fucked," I replied, which is true. He didn't seem that impressed with the vernacular and gave me a hard stare under his spectacle rims. "Gresik's having a look at them now, but I don't hold out much hope."

Before he had a chance to say anything else, I said, "I've come to see you about doing some sentry work. That's what I would have been doing in Katoomba if the place hadn't burnt to the ground. Besides which, I'm better at that than I am at putting bikes together."

"You're not just volunteering because of the extra food allowance are you?" he asked, although I'm quite sure he knew I wasn't.

"Not unless you're giving out burgers and fries," I replied. "No, if I'm going to be here, I'd rather you give me something to do that I'm good at instead of something I don't give a fuck about."

I felt I had to press my case a bit with Cullen, and in the end I got my way. He lined me up to go out with Than and Pete in the morning, which was fine with me.

After that, I came back here and had a nap. On the way, I passed some weedy-looking plant with a big blue flower and on a whim, I picked it. From what I've heard, chicks dig flowers.

Later, I heard Tahn and Lauren come back from wherever the fuck they've been for the last couple of days. I got up, slid the wine and glasses into a pack, slung it over my shoulder and went to their door with the flower in my hand. For the first time since we'd arrived in Katoomba, I had Topper's hat on, pulled down crookedly over one eye. I knocked.

Tahn opened the door and started laughing almost immediately. I looked past her at Lauren, who was trying to scowl but I looked so ridiculous that she smiled as well. For a moment we all stood there laughing. I gave Tahn the flower and she melodramatically sniffed it, then turned and handed it to Lauren.

"Thank you," she said with a smile that lit up her face. Under her mop of blond curls the effect was stunning. "Come in?"

"Got a better idea," I replied, and took her by the wrist.

We stopped by the dining room and she rustled us up a bit of a feed. There was, as usual, not much to pick from outside of kangaroo meat, rabbit, fish and a few handfuls of berrys and fruits and once again I was left to wonder just how well supplied the place really is. At least people won't be dying from obesity.

It was still an hour or so before dark so there was plenty of time for the climb. My uncle had brought me here once as a kid and we'd followed one of the trails to the

259

top of the ridge to where some bald rocks sat in a pile overlooking the valley. It would have probably been a strenuous walk once, but it seemed like nothing now. Tahnee looked impossibly delectable in the fading daylight. We talked and ate a little food as the stars began to come out in the east.

As I poured the wine, I told her I was sorry for hurting her. I'm sure she wanted me to say I was sorry for fucking Karen, and even though I am, it's not for the reason Tahnee wanted, so I didn't say it.

We didn't fuck right away. For a long time we lay next to each other, taking little sips of the surprisingly good wine and talking about different things like we had when we had been walking through the bush from Glenbrook and as the night got darker I pointed out a few constellations. Then she wriggled herself into my arms and we had long, slow sex like the kind they show in movies in soft focus with lingering shots of tangled bodies and entwined fingers. That's how it seemed, anyway. Quite special, unlike the bulk of my previous sexual experience. Maybe I really do feel something for this girl.

Time will tell, as it always does.

Monday October 8

I am pregnant. Dr Mcarthur told me last night. Tara just found out that she's pregnant too. I think that if I had found out I was pregnant two months ago, I would have totally freaked. I know I would have. But now I am happy and excited even though the doctor said I should be careful because I am so young and that the pregnancy might miscarry and it's so early that I shouldn't even really get excited yet. So yeah, I shouldn't be too excited but I can't help it. I have decided not to tell Talon yet. Plus, I don't know what he'll do or say if he finds out. But you know what? I don't care anyway. It's my baby.

Hee hee. That's a bit selfish.

Hey I just thought of a name. If it's a girl, I'm going to call her Hope.

Wednesday, October 10

Well it looks like the shit is really about to hit the fan. This is going to be a long entry because once again, as they have developed a habit of doing since the beginning of September, things have taken a bad turn. A little shy of noon today, Pete, Than and myself came across a girl in her late teens lying in the road next to a trail bike just outside the barricade on Caves Road. And she had some bad fucking news.

Earlier in the morning, two guys and a chick had headed off towards Edith in a small truck. They'd instigated the idea last night after a few of us, me included, got into a debate with Cullen about the level of resources and supplies we have. Despite his assurances, some of us aren't convinced there's enough to go around for that long and while there's a considerable risk in traipsing about the countryside, these three volunteered to go and spend a few days doing just that, with the idea that there's still a lot of non-perishable goods floating around in nearby hamlets simply waiting for someone to collect them. While he was reluctant, Cullen eventually relented and sent them off.

After what we've learned since, I hope they get back in one piece.

I met up with Pete and Than in the dining room for breakfast and afterwards talked them into having a heart-starter in the bar before we headed out on recon. Of course, old Lenny would have had a fit if he knew we were drinking so early, but I can't face the day without one so it was either that or I was going to be in a bad mood all day. The others knew this, and with a two hour hike ahead of us, they didn't want me in a bad mood.

We were about a kilometre from the barricade when we heard the bike approaching. I could tell it was a trail bike by the high-pitched buzz-saw whine of the engine. Even though we quickened our pace, it cut out before we got to the pile of cars and wire. Carefully, Pete scrambled over the wreckage. Once he'd reached the other side, he shouted for us to join him. As we lowered ourselves down from the bus to the ground on the other side, he was cradling a girl. Her eyes flickered open and after a second she started and flinched away from him violently. The bike was lying on the road as if she'd passed out and fallen off it, which was most likely the case.

In a moment she recovered her senses and looked up at us. Pete moved close to her again. She peered past him and looked at me with fear in her eyes. I went to take a step towards them but she flew into a panic and I thought better of it. It took a while for her to calm down so she was coherent, and while she did Than and Pete checked her over for injuries. There were none.

"Where did you just come from?" Pete asked her after a while.

She had started to breathe normally again but refused to look in my direction. Her dark hair was mussed and her face streaked with dirt and tears.

"Blackheath," she answered with a stammer. Then: "They killed everyone."

Pete looked up at me.

"Who? Who killed everyone?"

"Bikies! Murderers!" she cried, and I realised why I had frightened her. "A hundred of them or more, I don't know. They were everywhere. They found us and… and just started shooting everyone… My sister… I heard her screaming… they raped her and killed her… oh God!"

Pete helped her to her feet and he and Than steadied her as they led her to a stump on the roadside where she could sit. She was silent again for a while.

"You have to tell us what happened," Than said.

"OK, OK. Me and my sister, and some friends… we are from Blackheath. We have been there all this time. There was fourteen of us."

"Blackheath?" I asked, somewhat surprised. "We passed through there on the way here and didn't find a living soul."

"We were in the motel," she replied. "We knew you were there but there was just too many of you to challenge in the dark and we didn't know whether you were armed or what."

"I recognise you," she said, to Than. "We were going to try and speak to you the next day but when we saw you leaving we just let it be. We didn't really want anyone to know we were there. We thought it was safer for us if we just hid when people came. But today they found us… They came to the motel! I heard them. I hid. We all did but they found the others."

She started sobbing heavily and hyperventilating. Between bouts of this, she gradually explained that a hundred or so "bikies" and other miscreants had shown up early this morning and had then systematically rounded up her group, killing all the males immediately and then raping the women. Too scared to do anything else, she'd heard the screams as her sister and friends were passed around, used and then murdered. After an hour or so, she watched as the raiders slit the last girl's throat and then began ransacking shops. Then she'd managed to escape and make her way here. She didn't know why she'd come here.

"A lot of small groups had come through in the last few weeks but no one even bothered to look for us," she said at last. "After a while, I guess we just… just…"

"You just thought no one ever would," Pete said.

She nodded with a sob and fell silent. The three of us looked at each other, and we all saw the same look in return. This wasn't just bad. It was potentially catastrophic.

The girl fell to pieces. Pete radioed for the Landcruiser to come get us. Normally of course we would have walked back, but time was of the essence now. I thought about the team I'd argued so strongly in favour of sending out. I hoped they'd make it back and if they didn't, that it wasn't real obvious where they'd come from.

"This morning!" I said. "That means they could be here any minute!"

I doubted very much if they would be, though. Blackheath had still been pretty well in one piece when we'd left it a few days ago so I could only hope that they'd more than likely stay put for a while until they'd sucked the place dry before moving on to find another place to plunder. I know that's what I would do.

No doubt they'd pillage Mt Victoria next, and a handful of blokes with machine guns holed up in a pub probably wouldn't hold them off for very long, even if they are Army guys. Mt Vic is so small it's also possible they wouldn't even bother with the place unless they felt like trashing it just to let off some steam, which isn't out of the question.

Trying to predict their next move isn't going to be easy. If they're organised enough, they may even stay where they are and send out smaller parties until they find another decent target. Again, that's what I would do. And if chance brought me in this direction and I came roaring down the road and saw it blocked off with a big pile of cars and a warning sign with a smiley face painted on it, I'd attack just on principle.

We needed to get back to the village and get organised.

There is a chance that the outfit the girl had encountered this morning won't even come this way, especially when places like Lithgow, Portland and Oberon offer potentially more in the way of plunder. Then again, it's equally likely they might only be targetting small and isolated locations. Blackheath just happened to be convenient.

Apart from the barricades and booby traps, Cullen has been wise enough to at least plan a further defence strategy, and it's ok in theory. Being where we are, we have geography on our side, but all the caves, hidey-holes and elevated positions in the world will only prolong the inevitable unless people a) know how to fight, and b) are prepared to kill. Most people are ok with a). It's b) that causes the problems. I read somewhere once that up until the Vietnam War, even in close quarters fighting, American soldiers were more likely to just fire off random shots in the enemy's direction and hope they hit someone than make a deliberate killshot. I don't know how true that is, but I did hear an ANZAC veteran say just before he died that he believed that even after four years of trench warfare, he never fired directly at another human being.

That's the basic flaw in Cullen's plans. Apart from myself and Than, and possibly Farooq who apparently did some basic army training back in Pakistan, I'm not sure anyone else here has ever killed anyone or even so much as pointed a gun at someone. Except Tahnee, but that was in a blind rage, and her aim is lousy anyway. Pete and Clive were in the Army Reserve, which helps a bit, and some of the rest are or were farmers so they know which end of a gun is the dangerous one, but that's about it.

Back at the Caves, Cullen and Tara were waiting for us. Tara jumped into the car as the door opened to quickly check the girl over. Apart from being in a dead faint, she was apparently ok.

Tara helped Pete get her out and cart her off to the infirmary while Cullen accompanied Than and I to his office. The assortment of keys and other items stashed in little pouches hanging off his belt made a light jingle as he walked. He had so many that only someone as efficient as he could possibly remember what was in each one.

Inside the office, Greg was sitting on the desk wearing a faded shirt from some band I'd never heard of. Unlike the other times I'd seen him, he was wearing a pair of old army pants cut off just below the knee so I noticed for the first time that he had a picture of Dimebag from Pantera tattooed on his calf. As Cullen walked past him, he gave me a sheepish grin and slid off the table.

"Well gentlemen, what did our new visitor have to say?"

Cullen sat down in his chair sternly. I looked around for another chair, found one and slouched down in it, ignoring his gaze.

"She said that we're possibly in very deep shit," I said. Than nodded.

"Very deep," he agreed. "Hundred or so guys on bikes and cars. Heavy armed…"

"Bad attitudes. Just imagine a hundred of me, but worse."

Cullen nodded slowly. He may not have appreciated the way we'd expressed ourselves, but he understood it. He also understood that Than and I were probably the best qualified people to talk to about a potential attack.

"What kind of danger are we in, and what can we do about it?" he asked. Then he added with a wryness I didn't know he was capable of, "And it would be nice if you could elaborate a little."

"It all depends on how badly you want to hang on to this little community here," I began. "You've got the beginnings of a good thing going if you're able to keep it together through the winter though from what I've seen of the farm we're gonna be eating berries and ferntree hearts for a while yet and the booze is going to run out pretty soon. However, we're probably all doing better than if we were scattered all over the place in twos and threes. So, here's what I think. You can run like hell, or fight like fuck. I'm easy either way, but a hundred people can only run so far so fast for so long. I guess you could also barricade everyone up inside a cave until our friends have finished ransacking the place and razing everything to the ground and then come back out and try rebuilding, but I'm not real big on that idea."

Cullen nodded again.

"Than?" he said.

"We have good defendable position here. Many places to hide for ambush: up high, down low. Only trouble is not enough people who know how to fight, and not enough time to train. Going into battle is hard thing to do. Most people will just run away if they can."

"I know it would be hard for me," Greg offered. "I can handle myself in a scrap, but I don't know how I'd go with a hundred heavily armed goons charging at me even if I had a flamethrower. I could say now that I'd be fine, but when it actually happens," he shrugged, "I don't know what I'd actually do."

"Ever used a gun before?" I asked him. I was rather impressed that he'd been so honest in his self-assessment. Most people aren't.

"I shot a guy in the arse with a pellet gun once," he said, straight-faced, although I detected a self-deprecating tone that belied his expression. He shrugged again. "I was 11, and he was pissing me off. Not really much help I s'pose, but I know which end of a gun to point at someone. Whether I could actually pull the trigger, though… I don't know."

I was afraid it would be a similar story with almost everyone, though not all of them would be as frank.

Cullen looked slowly at each of us as we spoke, like a judge considering a verdict, which in a way is what he was. From the moment I'd laid on eyes on him, he had struck me as being a staunchly bureaucratic individual but one who was nonetheless capable of taking action decisively once he had all the details.

Yet all he did was look at me and ask, "What action would you take?"

I was surprised and found myself infuriated. It should have been obvious what to do. He didn't need to sit there and ask a guy who looked like a bandit what should happen next.

"You're in charge, Len," I told him. "You need to work out what you should do, not ask what I would do. Because what I would do is get myself a decent bike and ride on up to Blackheath, hitch my wagon to the anarchy train and go ravaging the countryside pillaging and deflowering nuns. Because that's a helluva lot easier than tilling a field, milking a cow and building a barn and trying to rebuild civilization from scratch with a bunch of people who only survived the Apocalypse in the first place because they were too fucking drunk to realise it was happening. There's no point asking me what I would do, because I'm a self-centred arsehole with allegiance to no one but me, myself and I. I don't need anything more than the clothes on my back, a handful of bullets and a bottle of whiskey with the prospect of a bit of pussy now and then to get me through the fucking day. You don't need to ask me what I should do. If you care about what you're building here, if you care about what happens to the people who are here and whatever future they might have in this righteously fucked-up world, then you already know what you have to do: You have to wait until you see the whites of their eyes, and then you have to murder every motherfucker that comes down that road. Because if you don't, they will tear this place apart and laugh while they do it, and anyone you leave alive will just come back pissed off."

There was a long silence in the room after that as Leonard Cullen and the others absorbed what I had said. Pete had come into the office during my rant and was looking at me like a stunned mullet. Greg was rubbing the back of his neck uncomfortably. Than was nodding numbly. It was more than possible that he'd experienced exactly the sort of thing I'd just described.

After a minute or so, Cullen finally spoke. He looked at me like I'd just picked him up out of his chair and shaken the crap out of him, but his voice sounded like I'd just said "Hello".

"We should probably get organised then," he said. "Greg, can you take these gentlemen to the armoury? They should be allowed to get some idea of what we have available."

I wondered what I'd have to say or do to get him to stop talking like he was in a board meeting.

We all turned to go but as I got to the door, Cullen called me back.

"There is one thing I do need to ask you, Talon," he said.

I knew what it would be.

"Why are you still here?"

"I don't know," I had to say, then I went out with the others.

It's true. I don't know why I'm sticking around. When I think about it, I don't even know why I left Sydney at all. It's quite likely that after the dust had settled from the shoot-out, big Spud might have come back to the gun store and we could have gone off together and found another bunch of reprobates to team up with. I wasn't exactly myself when I woke up after copping a bullet that day, and I pretty obviously haven't been myself ever since or I would have been out there cruising around like a pirate from then on. Tahnee's the sweetest tail I've ever had and if she lives long enough she'll make someone a great wife someday, but not me because I don't deserve her and I'll probably end up with my head blown off before I'm too much older in any case.

So that's not why I'm still here. It would be nice if it was, because even if I didn't understand why that was the reason, at least I'd know the reason. If I was religious at all or at least had some kind of belief in an afterlife, I could say that part of me is seeking redemption, but I'm not and I don't, and I've certainly never felt it necessary to be redeemed before. What I said to Cullen about not needing anyone is right, but it might also be, as I've written a couple of times before, that I just need to be needed. As I'm also sure I've written before, that sounds pretty stupid, but right now it also seems to make sense.

The armoury was a maintenance shed a short walk from the office. Whatever it had housed before had been replaced with a fairly impressive arsenal of hunting rifles and shotguns salvaged from Oberon's gun stores and nearby farmhouses. There was also boxes of explosives and bags of fertiliser and other things that could be used to make pipe bombs and homemade grenades.

At least we have plenty of firepower. I just hope there's enough time before we need to put it into use.

"Do you know how to make bombs, Than?" I asked.

"Yes," he replied sadly, with a sigh that said more than any words could that he had already killed more people than any sane person would ever wish to.

"Good. Then we better get started."

While he and Pete got to work shifting the bomb ingredients, Greg went off to round up a few helpers and I took stock of the hardware.

The gunstores around here were pretty well supplied by the look of it, at least so far as the types of legal firearms that farmers and shooters would normally use go. I've got little doubt that our friends in Blackheath probably have everything from Winchesters to AK47s at their disposal, and who knows what else, but even the peashooter I gave to Tahn will ruin your day if pointed at the right spot. Still, it would have been nice to see a couple of good assault rifles in the stockpile and I felt sure that if whomever had collected all of these had looked in the right spots, they would have found some. If only I'd been able to rescue some of the stuff we'd had in Katoomba.

Word spread pretty fast that there was the possibility of being massacred at any time, and even while I was still auditing the artillery, villagers began gathering in the square between the guest house and the office. A few started to demand to be told what was going on and a couple wanted to begin handing out weapons right away so they could go up into the hills and "pick off the bastards". When I asked one of them if he knew how to actually do that, he looked at me like he'd just caught me giving his wife the best orgasm of her life.

"Why don't we all just calm down a little?" I said. "I'm pretty sure that an army of cut-throats isn't about to come roaring out of the Grand Arch within the next few minutes, because if it were you'd be watching my back disappearing over that hill. It's likely that a few bad guys might try to stop by in the next few days, but grabbing a rifle and running off into the bush shooting at anything that moves is going to cause more problems than it solves."

I didn't just write that because it sounds cool. That's what I really said.

I should have been a politician.

With the help of some people who knew me from Katoomba, I got the crowd settled, but even so everyone was on edge. That's understandable, because while I really don't think the danger is immediate, or even imminent, it's very real. Various versions of the morning's atrocity had crept through the village like Chinese whispers and everyone seemed very afraid.

As Cullen came out toward me and people quietened, I

took a good look at them all for the first time. Most were beginning to go nut-brown from working in the open all day. Many were lean or leaner than they'd once been and several were starting to look gaunt. They were all shapes and sizes, Anglos, a few Asians, an Indian, a couple of Arabs, an Aboriginal guy, some Europeans of various origin. The wretches of the First Fleet probably didn't look that different after a few weeks of inadequate food and hard labour, except for the t-shirts. And at least they had Marines armed with muskets to ward off any Stone Age marauders carrying spears and clubs. This lot were going to have to use .22s against motherfuckers with machine guns. Looking at them, I wondered again why I was even bothering.

When winter comes, most of these poor bastards will probably die of starvation.

St. Jude has got nothing on me.

Cullen was patient with the agitated crowd. He explained defence strategies, answered questions and designated tasks. He didn't gloss over things and he didn't lie. For people to be able to prepare for a threat, they had to know exactly what the threat was. His language wasn't as colourful as mine had been, but he let them know that if anyone tried to invade, we'd have to make sure we killed them all. I wasn't sure that what he said would be enough to ensure that these ordinary people would be able to do what was required, but in the absence of a bloke in a kilt with half his face painted blue spouting rhetoric from horseback, it was the best we could do.

When he was finished and the crowd had dispersed, worried but informed and aware of what was required from each of them, Cullen turned to me once more.

"I have something else to ask you now," he said. "Are you going to stick around and help?"

"I don't know," I said again. "I've fucked off on people before."

Then I picked up a couple of rifles and walked away.

Cullen's words still ring in my ears as I sit here now watching Tahnee's tits move up and down as she sleeps. "Just like Katoomba," he said.

Just like fucking Katoomba. Fuck yes. Why not? I'm not Shane. I'm not Max Rockatansky. I haven't got a sense of honour making me stick around to help hopeless causes. Today I saw a woman holding a newborn baby. What fucking chance does she have, even if we wipe out every badass fucker left on the planet? She might as well take her little bundle, fill her shoes with stones and drop herself into the Blue Lake like Virginia Woolf. At least she'll die quickly that way.

Thursday, October 11

I was going to tell Talon yesterday, but I'm scared that if I tell him now he'll leave for sure and make me go too. Maybe we should leave, but not yet. He has to stay and help everyone fight. After that if we're still alive I'll tell him and if he wants to I'll go wherever he wants.

I'm scared about the fight too. Everything's been so good and quiet since we got here that I almost forgot how bad it is out there and how many bad people there must still be going around killing and raping and destroying things. Me and Lauren talked once about just finding a little farm far away from everything one day and living there but what if we had done that and some one had come along and attacked us? That must of happened a lot to the early settlers and it's kind of like those days all over again now, or more like in one of those old Western movies that I used to watch when I was little and off school with the flu. They would always have some bandits or Indians attacking a farmhouse or a little town or something. Except the army or some good guys would come and fight them off. Now there's no army and the only good guys that can fight is us.

Well I might be scared, but I'm going to fight hard. My dad taught me how to shoot and now that I've got a little person growing inside me I'm not going to let some greasy fucker get his hands on me. I will fucking kill anyone who tries it.

After Talon shot those kids that were going to rape me that day I asked him how he could just blow them away like that and he told me that he just does what he has to and doesn't even think about it. I said that I didn't think I could be like that and he said that I probably would have to be from now on. Well I guess that now I do. I nearly shot Talon by accident so if I can do that then I reckon that I could shoot someone on purpose.

I read about some kids who took guns to school one day and just started shooting everyone and when the cops finally got them and asked them how they could have done that, they just said that they were pretending they were in a video game. That's pretty fucked up shooting other kids at school for no reason, but I think that when the attack happens if I need to I can just imagine I'm in a game too.

Maybe I will feel bad or feel sick after, but at least I will still be alive. I wrote in here once that I didn't want to live anymore. Now I want to live more than ever. I want to be a mum like Mary. Even if something real bad happens and I lose this one before it's born, I know that I want to be a mum and have a baby. Maybe have two or three and bring them up to help start the world all over again. That might be why I am still alive. That's why I have to do whatever I have to do to protect myself from now on.

I'm going out to do some shooting practice with this rifle that Greg gave me. When the time comes, I'm going to kickass.

I'd never had a chance to develop a defence for Katoomba, and in retrospect even with the wall I'd been so stupidly proud of, it probably would have eventually come down to close combat in the main street. It was an impossible place to hold off a concerted raid by anything more than a handful of assailants. Than is right though. Here at Jenolan the chances are better. Indeed, a well-trained unit with good local knowledge could hold off an invasion here for months. Military training might be thin on the ground, but at least local knowledge isn't non-existent.

Cullen and some of the others who used to work here know the place like the backs of their hands and, to their credit, had long identified the best defensive positions even before any refugees had started drifting into the place. They were also aware that a barricade of car wrecks and razor-wire, even a booby-trapped one, wouldn't hold off determined invaders but it did at the very least provide an obstacle that would allow time to prepare for their arrival. Now that we have groups watching the roads further out, there should be even more time.

When the heat's on, I'm sure there'll be some fight among us. A few might run off into the bush or piss themselves or both, but back at the Carrington I'd seen guys who looked like they'd never even been in a bad mood in their lives pick up guns and point them murderously at people, so there's a good chance at least a few of those here will offer resistance. The biggest worry is when an attack will come, and from which direction. It could be days away, or it could be before I finish writing this sentence. And it could be from the north, which is easier to defend against, or it could be from the west, or it could be from both directions at once. Again, the groups watching the roads should give ample warning. I just hope to shit it's not a two-pronged attack.

It's also hard to say how big the enemy is. The girl from Blackheath said there was a hundred or so, but she was terrified and running for her life so she probably didn't stick around long enough to count them. As a rough figure even that's a shitload of cut-throats to go up against, but there's no way of knowing if that's all there is or if that group wasn't just a forward party for a fuckload more. If that's the case, we don't even stand the ghost of a chance that we do now, and if it is, I've already put Tahnee and Lauren on notice that I won't be hanging around to watch the fun.

Tahnee should get the fuck out anyway. If she isn't throwing her cunt up every day from morning sickness then I'm a cross-dressing fag. This is no place for a pregnant teenage girl, and wouldn't be even if a thousand killers and rapists weren't about to descend on it. She probably hasn't told me yet because she doesn't want me to worry – or doesn't know she's pregnant, which isn't likely. I'd hardly be surprised considering how often we fuck and now she's got the taste for it she wants it more than I do. Anyway, it doesn't concern me whether she's up the duff or not.

I fathered a child once before, or so I was told. I fucked some slut at a mate's 18th birthday party and a couple of months later her dad pounds on the door of my flat, threatening violence because I'd knocked up his kid. After I told him that it could have been any number of people, he got cranky and I eventually had to bash him with a spanner. Six weeks after that, they threw me in the can for assault and that's where I met Scooter and Gonk. I never saw the slut again, or her sprog at all, and because I started using the name Talon after I got out instead of my real name, I never heard from her again either and until now I doubt I've thought about her in ten years. They'd both most likely be dead now anyway. And her dad.

The possibility of becoming a father once again, if I even had been previously, doesn't exactly fill me with joy right now. Maybe I'd feel good about it if the end of the world hadn't come along, but now there doesn't seem to be much point.

Well, I rambled a bit there. If I'm going to keep on with this log even with all hell about to break loose at any moment, I should probably stop doing that.

Most of the men have been given weapons now and divided up into small units. Some of the women too: Tahnee, Lauren, Paula, Tara, Nurse Ratched ("I'll blow their fucking heads off," she'd said like some living, breathing cliché), Angela the bar maid. No use being sexist. Pete, Clive, Than and Farooq will be leading a group each. Everyone else including the doctor will be holing up in the Cathedral chamber in the Lucas Cave. Cullen's going in there too. He was dead against it, but eventually I convinced him that if the rest of us are massacred, someone's going to have to lead the survivors. Plus, if they're going to be hiding away in a cave, they should be with someone who knows their way around.

To help provide an advanced warning to an attack, Cullen had nominated four teams of two to head out to points along the roads to keep watch. One team is in Hampton, a little hamlet nestled under a hill on a curve of the road from the north near the turn-off to Oberon. Another is at Edith, keeping an eye on the way in from the west. Each team is to be relieved by another just before dawn every day. Providing they see the enemy before the enemy sees them, that should give us ten to fifteen minutes to prepare if an attack comes.

I keep writing 'if', but I know in my heart that it's more of a 'when'. When it does come, it's going to be brutal.

We'll probably be slaughtered.

Saturday, October 20

I wasn't sure when or if I was going to pick up this book and write in it ever again, and after today I probably won't. I can move my left arm now and when I can get it fully mobile again I'll most likely be on my way. Gresik's patched up this really nice chopper that Taylor found so once I can ride it there'll be no holding me back. I should close the chapter though, so to speak. But I'm thinking that it might not be that easy.

For three days everyone was on edge. A few people tried to make the best of it, but it's hard to put on a brave face when the possibility of that face being blown off at any time is hanging over one's head. People carried their rifles constantly, even after Cullen asked them all to keep them secure. Many at least made themselves useful and spent an hour or so each day shooting targets and learning how to pull them apart, clean them and load them.

Cullen and I got together with the others we'd designated as unit leaders and pored over tactics until we ran out of ideas. In the end, we developed what we finally agreed was the best possible plan.

Pete's group would be positioned under Carlotta Arch, outside the entrance to the Arch Cave. High above the road, it provides excellent views across the valley that leads here. Farooq's unit would hide themselves in the mouth of the Nettle Cave and among the boulders around the eastern end of the Devils Coachhouse. Than would take some guys and go into hiding somewhere north of Jenolan along the road. My team would be inside the Grand Arch, with half protecting the Lucas Cave side and the rest on the Chifley Cave side. Clive would have his unit scattered through the buildings in the village. The overall plan was for the forward teams to funnel the invaders into the Grand Arch and then pin them from all sides: Pete from above, Farooq from the left and myself from the front, with Than's group making a sneak attack from the rear. With any luck the bulk of the invaders would be stopped then and there and any that got through could then be bombarded with pipe bombs from Clive's team.

We figured it was the best tactic, because once inside the Grand Arch, there's no way to turn around. Anyone who got as far as the tunnel would have to keep going right through to be picked off at the other end. I couldn't help thinking that anyone coming here would realise the possibility for such an ambush almost immediately and take steps to defend against it, but I also knew that the army of thugs that the girl from Blackheath had described was most likely to act under the impression that their very numbers would be enough to win half the battle, and the only real attack strategy they would have would be to launch an intimidating-looking charge into a place and start shooting it up. If that was the case, then it was definitely possible that we could use such brazenness to our advantage. The major concern though was that under decent leadership, a large body of attackers could in fact divide somewhere and come in from both directions at once, or even not come from the north at all and attack from the west instead, where the road snakes down into the village from above, making it harder to defend.

In the end, it turned out that they did come out of the north after all, so the plans we made for the other possibilities are irrelevant now.

Much like plans for just about everything else, really, when you think about it.

Anyway, as I said, for three days nothing happened. The party that had gone out in the truck came back, loaded with goodies they'd pilfered from various dots on the map all over the countryside. They hadn't seen anything more than scattered groups in twos and threes ekeing out new lives from isolated farmhouses. All three of them volunteered to take on an attack.

Just before dawn on the 15th , Taylor and a girl called Carly rode out to Hampton to relieve the scouts there. That pair had just had time to get back here when Carly called in. An army of bikes and trucks roared into the hamlet and halted there, virtually right under where she had taken up position. A short time later, Taylor saw ten or twelve riders pass by his post at the junction with the Oberon Road, heading in different directions.

Pete came to collect me, and I hadn't needed to ask why. Cullen was already in the office when I got there.

"They're on their way," he said ominously.

Ten or fifteen minutes went by. Then the radio crackled into life.

"Hello down there," said a voice like a screeching violin. "Have we got a fucking surprise for you!"

There was laughter.

"A big, big fucking surprise!" Mr. Damage cackled. "Have a nice day!"

The radio went dead. He had no way of knowing that it wasn't that much of a surprise, but at least the motherfucker had the decency to warn us.

I wanted to call Taylor back and ask him to tell us when they went past again, but I knew that they'd probably be listening and I couldn't risk them finding him. If he did what he was supposed to do, and I felt sure that he would, he'd keep silent until they actually got rolling. I had no doubt the whole lot of them would descend on the place.

In hindsight, they were a lot like the kids in the arena. They had been so intent on having their lustful adolescent way with Tahnee that they had neither thought to go through our belongings to find anything useful nor considered the fact that I was one dangerous bastard who could waste them all without a moment's thought. These guys were obviously so driven in their pursuit of plunder and pussy that they completely ignored the possibility of meeting organised resistance from a group of people in an extremely defendable location.

I found myself wondering if I would have fallen victim to that mob mentality if I had been with them, instead of being here, and I realised that it was highly possible.

We swung into action. The sick and the weak had been taken into the Cathedral days ago, so all that was left was to get Cullen and the others who weren't going to be doing any killing there too. Than's unit was on the road within minutes. I had to hand it to him, for in a couple of days he'd knocked them into good shape. They didn't even wait for the rest of us to get ready. Pete and Farooq took their squads and got into position. Clive's team had collected on the porch of the guesthouse. Apart from Tara, who looked like the kind of woman who wouldn't back down from anything and take shit from no one, they were the ones I had least confidence in. They were the last line of defense. I had to make sure that they knew it was imperative that the moment they saw anything hostile come through the Arch, it had to be destroyed.

"It will be," Tara said, as if she spoke for them all. Perhaps she did, but I still wasn't wholly convinced.

It was half an hour or more before Taylor called to say that the attack was imminent. Lock, stock and barrell, the entire army had pulled up stumps and was heading down Caves Road toward us.

A few minutes later a series of blasts rocked the valley as the invaders reached the barricade and evidently bombed it until they could pass through. After that, we didn't have to wait much longer.

The throaty rumble of Harley Davidsons that had been such music to my ears for years filled the valley. Obviously, the booby-traps scattered around the road had been utterly ineffectual.

I looked around at my squad and all of them were terrified.

"Get ready!" I cried.

Lauren had the two-way hanging from her belt. Somewhat needlessly, I heard Pete declare "Here they come!" and, indeed, here they came.

The first wave of attackers broke from the trees and hurtled toward us. If they were expecting an ambush, they didn't show any sign.

As the first of them roared across the gap between the trees and the bridge, I lined up the closest one I could get a bead on and brought him to the ground with a shot through the heart. I heard someone else open fire from the mouth of the Nettle Cave and I swore. I only hoped that the other units would hold their fire until the attackers got closer. None of them seemed to take any notice of the shot though and they kept straight on.

They weren't all bikers. Some of them were just evil-looking dudes who'd probably been stand-over men or wife-beaters in a previous life. Others could have been leftovers from the group me and the boys had taken on in the gun store and there was one or two that looked like otherwise normal blokes who'd thrown their lot in with these thugs to avoid having their throats cut. I wasn't that surprised to see a couple of the goons Mitchell had gathered to himself in Katoomba, although I didn't see him anywhere. There was a sprinkling of women among them too, mostly total skanks that even Pretty Boy wouldn't have fucked. Almost every rider had a pillion armed with some variety of automatic weapon.

If the invaders had been under the impression that their overwhelming superiority in numbers and firepower would have been enough for them to have taken over the place in seconds, they were about to have that belief shattered.

I heard Greg yell above the din of engines and gunfire erupted from the southern side of the cave. An ugly looking bastard at the front of the charge caught a volley full in the chest. He cannoned backwards off his bike and collided with a guy behind him who had just pulled the pin from a grenade with his teeth. They hit the tarmac together as their riderless bikes speared off into the paths of several others. Riders swerved and veered to miss them. Then the grenade bounced and went off in mid-air with a blinding explosion that decapitated one guy and eviscerated another two while sending pieces of hot metal in all directions. Another three goons crumpled lifeless to the ground, their bikes roaring on without them. One of our young blokes had put himself too far forward and collapsed without a sound.

Another grenade skittered under a fire tanker that had been parked on the southern side of the Arch to provide cover. It went off with a dull crumping sound. The truck lifted slightly as its back broke and both the fuel and water tanks ruptured, unleashing a deluge that raced over the roadway and plunged into the creek.

More bikes screamed into the clearing, led by a fat dude with an eagle tattooed across his bulk. He opened up with a machine gun, raking the front of the Arch and sending a couple of defenders scattering. One of them fell and didn't get back up. A rifle shot from up high took most of Fatty's head away and he plowed into a bike beside him, sending it careering off the road. It hit a tree stump and the rider was thrown headlong, screaming as he cartwheeled through the air into a boulder.

I'd only let one shot off so far, and already there were

attackers lying in bloody pieces all over the road. It was an impressive start. Now all we had to do was maintain it.

The truck which had copped the grenade strike suddenly erupted loudly. A sheet of flames raced across the roadway outside as fire danced along the diesel slick. Thick black smoke began to billow from the mouth of the Arch.

Bikes plunged headlong into the Arch. Thugs began firing off shots in random directions around the place, seemingly oblivious to the possibility that they were being funnelled into it to be picked off more easily. A small volley impacted into the limestone close to my head and I dropped. From the corner of my eye I saw Tahnee lean out from cover and take a bead on a chick in a yellow bikini riding pillion to an enormous guy who looked like Shrek. She was waving a revolver around, firing wildly and whooping like Annie Oakley.

Tahnee blew her brains out just as it struck me who they both were. The Shrek-looking individual – Spud – just kept right on as if he was bulletproof. He didn't even realise the girl, the slut from the Terminus Est house, had given her last bad blowie. He didn't even look around. The surreality of the situation left me spellbound for a moment, until another burst of gunfire broke my reverie.

"Fucking bitch!" I heard Tahn say, then she dived for

cover as a spray of hot lead bounced around the roof of the cavern.

A weedy guy wearing a bandana leapt off the back of a big fat Triumph and began running up the stairs. He had a knife between his teeth like a pirate and looked so idiotic that I laughed as blew him away. Several other bandits had pulled the same stunt. They were scrambling up the rocks towards the Lucas Cave entrance where Greg, Drew, Paula and several others had so far been holding their own. Unlike the raiders though, they weren't killers and I wondered how they'd go now their battle was about to move from firing at a group en masse and hoping to score a few hits to making sure every shot counted.

More and more bikes rumbled down the roadway and began roaring toward the caves. Their passengers were doing the bulk of the shooting as they approached. While they weren't being particular where they fired, they had full automatic weapons so they didn't need to be that precise. Behind them I could see some four-wheel drive utes with belt-fed machine guns mounted on their roofs and a couple of Army trucks with fuck knows what ordinance in them. They were in view of our positions but weren't moving toward us. I could only hope that Than's unit was ready to give them a couple of pipe bombs to welcome them to the party.

As the riders at the back of the pack rumbled toward the

Arch, defenders opened fire from everywhere and cut them to pieces in a crossfire that would have impressed Sam Peckinpah. Bodies fell and bikes went in all directions. The road was littered with the dead and dying, with shattered motorbikes and discarded weaponry. Someone lobbed a Molotov cocktail from the direction of the Devils Coachhouse, igniting fuel leaking from holed petrol tanks. There was a loud woofing noise followed by a chorus of screams that must be something like Dante heard in Hell.

Surviving riders were still pouring through the Arch, disgorging passengers and racing through to the other side. Most of the pillions were gunned down before they could take their feet, but a few managed to make cover and return fire. A guy beside me whose named I remembered only as Marcus fell forward with a hole in his throat I could have put my fist in. Tahnee barked in pain as a bullet grazed her shoulder. She sloughed it off and took aim at a guy dressed like he'd just stepped out of the dingiest night club that had ever existed. The shot went slightly wide but it got his attention enough for him to turn towards her, but as he did someone killed him. What had to be one of the world's ugliest women had climbed onto the roof of the toilet block and was about to lob a grenade when Greg and Drew both fired simultaneously, cutting her down with a shriek before she could pull the pin.

From the other end of the tunnel I heard an explosion, and could only hope that Clive, Tara and the others were throwing pipe bombs at anything coming out into the daylight as they'd been told to do. They weren't killers either though, so I couldn't be sure that the blasts I heard hadn't been the handiwork of Spud or his mates.

Inside the cave, the battle subsided. I put binoculars up to my face and watched a couple of dozen guys dressed in a combination of leathers and Army fatigues scramble over the 4WDs. One of them was an enormous Chevy that had been armoured with thick plating that looked like battleship iron and had the blade off a grader bolted in place below the bullbar. Something told me that such a ridiculously reinforced vehicle could only belong to whomever was leading this little army.

Just as I was wondering what Than could possibly have been doing all this time, one of the Army trucks brewed up and exploded and I watched flashes of gunfire break out among the trees.

I jumped down onto the roadway and shouted for everyone to follow me. Greg, Paula, Tahnee, Lauren, Drew and two or three others were all miraculously still in one piece and apart from looking a bit traumatised, a few light wounds from shrapnel and grime from sweat, they seemed to be ok. Greg, whose supply of band tees appears strangely unlimited, had an Alice Cooper tour shirt wrapped around his head, staunching the flow from a bullet graze.

"Let's go," I said and started moving toward the battle at the other end of the cave. There was a little bit too much fighting going on from that direction for something that should have ended with a couple of well-placed pipe bombs.

Before we could get far, however, the crossfire behind us started up again. I spun around to see the hideous Chevy laying rubber and rocketing toward the Grand Arch like the ugliest missile of all time.

I scooped up an AK-47 that some dead guy had no further use for.

"Fucking scatter!" I yelled at the others and all of them did except Drew, who also picked up a machine gun. Ever since I'd set him straight about who was the man and who was the boy, he'd been hanging around me and carrying on like a disciple, so it didn't wholly surprise me that he was so eager to help out once again. As he'd never fired a machine gun before, his action was pure folly and could potentially get him killed, but I didn't have time to argue.

The Chevy was already halfway to the cave mouth. Pete and Farooq's units were unloading everything they had at it. The suicide who'd been manning the gun on the roof was shot to ribbons almost instantly but the truck itself received nothing more than hollow dents.

At first I panicked, and fired off a volley of shots that bounced in all directions off the grader blade and the metal plates that had reduced the windscreen to a narrow slit. Then people started shouting and shooting from behind me and I realised that the others were blazing away at the truck as well. I leapt aside, firing, as it plunged into the Arch and somehow managed to shoot away both back tyres. The rims bounced off the roadway with a shower of sparks and a scream like King Kong's nails down a blackboard and the Chevy lurched to one side and flipped. It slid a few metres and slammed into the limestone, breaking in two. The heavily armoured cab rolled with a metallic groan and landed on its wheels.

I got to my feet and walked over to the wreck. It was pretty unlikely anyone inside had been wearing a seat belt, so I was fairly sure no one could have survived a crash like that, and if they did then they'd hardly be in a position to pull a gun. I grabbed the door and wrenched it open.

Inside, Ronald Parry was looking at me. For some reason, I wasn't the least bit surprised.

"You fuck," he said, spitting blood. More than in a bad way, he looked as though he'd been thrown into a tumble dryer with a brick and an iron bar.

"Look who's talking," I replied. Then I fired the AK at him.

I stepped back from the truck and Lauren pressed the radio into my hand.

"Talon! Are you there? It's Farooq."

"Go ahead," I said.

"Oh good, you're still alive! I'm going to move out and help Than."

"We'll cover you from up here!" Pete offered.

"Go for your life," I said. "Just watch out for those heavy machine guns."

I tried to raise Clive, but got only silence. The gunfire on his side of the ridge had dwindled from frantic to sporadic, but it was hard to say what that could mean. Greg was anxious to go and check. We headed for the end of the tunnel, with Greg and Drew a little ahead. Keeping to the shadows as we got close to the cave mouth, I pulled the others up so I could scan the landscape.

The shattered remains of man and machine lay strewn over the roadway between the Arch and the buildings. All gunfire had completely ceased and by the look of it there was no one left to cause any. I carefully moved forward into the sun, giving me a better view of the scene. On the road outside the guest house, I saw someone raise an arm and heard them cry out weakly. It was Tara. She appeared to be trying to drag herself back inside. The black dog was standing beside her, looking hopelessly lost and frightened.

The other bodies scattered around displayed no signs of life. I knew Greg would be aching to get to his wife.

I sent Drew with Greg to give him cover, telling them to move carefully and quickly and to keep as close to the cliff as possible. Tahnee, Paula and I slipped further out from the cave and kept watch over them as they moved in a crouching run toward where Tara lay. They reached her without incident and Greg helped her to her feet. She wasn't able to stand by herself. Hobbling and clutching him tightly, she went with him into the building. Drew threw an "OK" sign.

Walking slightly in front, I led the others in a line six abreast toward the guesthouse. The carnage was far less than what I'd witnessed on the other side of the ridge, but it was clear the fighting had been no less intense. By the look of some of the ragdolls laying around the place, at least one pipe bomb and possibly two had been put to good use. Every ground level window in the office building and several in Caves House had been blown or shot out.

I reached the shell of a guy who was oozing blood from a hole in his back and kicked him. He wouldn't be giving us any trouble.

"Keep your eyes open," I warned. The closer we got to the guesthouse, the more likely it was that someone could jump out from somewhere.

Which is exactly what did happen. I saw the movement

and heard the noise just a fraction too late. A large shape suddenly kicked its way through a door and swept the area with a spray of automatic fire.

A slug tore through my left shoulder and I howled in pain. Behind me, I heard Lauren scream.

The bullet threw me violently to the ground. Pain swept over me like a flood. It felt like someone had driven a white-hot iron rod through me. I couldn't move or even think, but that only lasted a moment. Whoever had shot me was only a few metres away and not very likely to suddenly drop his weapon and run away screaming.

I raised myself slightly with my good arm and shook my head to clear it.

Tahnee was lying on the road beside me. I didn't need to look at her twice to know that she was never going to get up again. Lauren had seen this too, and began wailing in anguish.

In spite of everything, I reached out and brushed Tahnee Goss gently on the cheek.

Then a shadow fell across me and I looked up.

Just as I had known who it was I would find in the cab of the Chevy, I knew who I'd see now.

Good old explosion-loving, Tahnee-murdering, Spud motherfucking McConnell loomed over me from barely two metres away.

He seemed to suddenly realise who I was. His face changed from a blank slate to that big, dumb look he used to get when the punchline of a joke from five minutes before finally registered.

"Talon..?"

"Spud," I said. "You're a motherfucker."

Charging at him from behind, Drew opened fire and cut him in half.

I rolled onto my side, threw my arm over Tahnee, sweet, dead Tahnee, and cried until I passed out.

They thought I had died then. I don't know why I didn't. I can't even begin to know why I managed to pull through while Tahnee lays in the cold earth, her newfound hopes for the future gone forever as if they'd never existed.

A few days ago I wrote that I didn't think I was capable of love, but I loved that girl like the sun loves to shine. If anyone deserved to make it through this, it was Tahnee. She could have made it through almost anything, and in a way she did.

I pulled the photo of her with Mary's baby out of her book and put it into my little box with a lock of her hair. One day someone might find it resting next to my skeleton.

Before I leave, I'm going to give both our diaries to Cullen, so that if what's left of humanity here in this little valley ever manages to claw its way back to a semblance of civilization, someone someday will know how it all went down.

The doctor says I won't be able to travel for a few weeks, and he's not lying. The big chopper Taylor salvaged for me from the destruction is going to need two fit arms to keep it under control. But I'm in no hurry. I never was.

Tara's ok, but she'll have trouble walking for a while. Clive bought it though, and Than was killed in the sneak attack on the trucks. Most of the rest made it, although some of them will have some nice scars to show off one day. They're probably through with killing though, even if the killing isn't through with them. They've survived this battle, but there's a long dark tunnel ahead.

Perhaps someone will reach the end of it eventually.

www.ingramcontent.com/pod-product-compliance
Lightning Source LLC
Chambersburg PA
CBHW072123020726
47501CB00003B/946